THE BOY I

MW00938694

A Psychological Thriller

BY DITTER KELLEN

Subscribe to Ditter's Newsletter for free books, new release alerts and contest opportunities!

<u>Sign Me Up!</u>

Copyright © by Ditter Kellen

All rights reserved. This copy is intended for the original purchaser of this e-book ONLY. No part of this e-book may be reproduced, scanned, or distributed in any printed or electronic form without prior written permission from Ditter Kellen. Please do not participate in or encourage piracy of copyrighted materials in violation of the author's rights. Purchase only authorized editions.

Image/art disclaimer: Licensed material is being used for illustrative purposes only. Any person depicted in the licensed material is a model.

Published in the United States of America.

This e-book is a work of fiction. While reference might be made to actual historical events or existing locations, the names, characters, places and incidents are either the product of the author's imagination or are used fictitiously, and any resemblance to actual persons, living or dead, business establishments, events, or locales are entirely coincidental.

Warning

This e-book contains adult language and situations that may be considered offensive to some readers. This e-book is for sale to adults ONLY as defined by the laws of the country in which you made your purchase. Please store your files wisely where they cannot be accessed by under-aged readers.

Dedication

This book is dedicated to my editor and friend, Johnny Mack. Since telling him of this story, he has pushed me to finish it. I hope I do him proud.

Acknowledgments

I would like to acknowledge a few people who mean a lot to me, and who's continued love and support have helped to make this happen.

Cathe Green is a rock. She's been a close friend for many years. She reads my stories, tells me where I went wrong or right, and she never wavers in her devotion. I love you, Cathe!

Amy Bingham is a Godsend. She's smart, funny and carries the load for me more times than I can count. She's become a great friend whom I love with all my heart.

My tribe…Thank you ladies for the shares, the laughs and for loving my babies. I've come to think of you all as family and I appreciate everything you do for me.

My husband...my Beast...my biggest fan. I love you more than my breath. Never forget that.

Chapter One

"Are you still not sleeping?"

Jessica Nobles shook her head numbly and lifted her gaze to Dr. Knox. "The dreams keep me up at night. Even with medication, I wake up terrified."

Her husband Owen reached for her hand, but she pulled away, her attention focused on the doctor. "With every dream I have, Jacob's face disappears a little more."

Leonard Knox leaned back in his chair and stared at her through the lenses of his glasses. "Any more suicidal thoughts?"

Jessica swallowed around a throat gone dry. "Sometimes. I haven't acted on any of them, but the thoughts still cross my mind."

"It's been three years since your son's passing, Mrs. Nobles. I understand your grief, truly, I do. But at this point, your psychiatrist and I both feel that continued sedation could be doing more harm than good."

"You understand my grief?" Jessica's anxiety quickly replaced her numbness. "How can you sit there and say that? You've never lost a child."

"Jess…" Owen reached for her hand once again, only to pull back when she yanked free of his hold.

She took a shuddering breath, unable to look away from the doctor's sympathetic gaze. "When Jacob died…I wanted to die right along with him. You have no idea what it's like to go on living when everything you've ever lived for is gone."

Owen visibly flinched next to her.

"You're right, Mrs. Nobles," the doctor admitted in a soft tone. "I've never lost a child. However, I do understand loss. It's true that everyone processes grief in their own way, but it's been three years. We should be seeing progression not regression."

"I'm doing the best I can…"

Propping his elbows on his desktop, the doctor murmured, "You have to stop blaming yourself for your son's death. There was nothing you could have done to save him."

"Had I been home to get him off the school bus, he wouldn't have been hit by that oncoming car."

Doctor Knox shook his head. "The driver of that car was drunk. There was nothing you could have done to stop him."

Jessica's mind processed the doctor's words, but the guilt she felt at not being there when Jacob had stepped off that bus still remained. "I guess we'll never know, will we?"

"My goal here is to help you cope with your pain," the doctor persisted. "The medication previously prescribed by your psychiatrist was meant as a temporary form of relief, not a long-term fix."

Before Jessica could respond, the doctor shifted his attention to Owen. "How are things at home?"

"About the same." Owen cleared his throat and continued, "The fighting has lessened a bit, but the intimacy is still nonexistent."

Jessica stared straight ahead, listening to Owen and the doctor speak about her as if she wasn't there.

She and her husband had been seeing Doctor Knox, along with a psychiatrist, since their seven-year-old son's death three years ago.

Though Owen had taken Jacob's death extremely hard, he'd somehow managed to cope without medications. Not Jessica. Her mind had crawled into a dark place she couldn't seem to come back from.

"Perhaps you should consider packing up Jacob's things and storing them somewhere else. It won't remove the pain you're feeling from his loss, but it would be a huge step in moving on with your lives."

Jessica's heart stuttered, her mind rebelling against the doctor's words.

Owen spoke up before she could form a response. "I feel that it's time as well. I've been offered a position at another bank, which means I would be transferred. I—"

"Another bank?" Jessica interrupted, cutting off the rest of Owen's words. "This is the first I've heard of it. Transferred to where?"

Shifting on his seat to face her, Owen stated quietly, "Florida."

Jessica jumped to her feet, enraged that her husband hadn't mentioned anything to her about a transfer before their appointment with Knox.

She marched toward the door, only to come up short when Owen appeared in front of her.

He gently gripped her by the shoulders. "Please don't do this, Jess. Just hear me out."

"When were you planning on telling me?" she shot back, ignoring the fact that Doctor Knox witnessed their squabble.

Owen's hands fell away. "I only found out myself yesterday."

"So, you thought it would be best to drop that bomb on me while we were here where I wouldn't show my temper? Think again." She stepped around him, jerked the door open, and fled the room.

Owen caught up with her at the elevators. His face appeared pale and moisture gathered in his light blue eyes. "I lost him too, Jess."

Pain penetrated Jessica's heart; the horror of losing Jacob sliding through her anew. No matter how much time had passed since his death, she couldn't seem to get beyond the realization that he was truly gone. "Then how can you even consider moving from Chicago—from the only home our son ever knew?"

"Jacob's gone, Jess. He's not coming back. It's time we get on with our lives before I lose you, too."

Nausea rolled, nearly doubling Jessica over. She slapped a hand over her mouth and repeatedly pressed the button to the elevator. She needed to get as far away from Owen as she could. He'd betrayed her, plotting a move behind her back—a move that would take her far away from Jacob's home, his memories...his grave.

Chapter Two

The living room light shone through the rain as Jessica pulled into the drive of her two-story home on Jenson Street.

She put the small SUV in park, switched off the engine, and leaned her head against the seat back to listen to the storm.

Owen would be up; no doubt worried sick. He'd been calling her every ten minutes since she'd practically ran from Dr. Knox's office earlier that afternoon.

Jessica had driven around for hours in the freezing weather, weeping, until she'd found herself at the cemetery kneeling in front of her son's grave.

She wasn't sure how much time had passed with her begging Jacob to forgive her for not being there for him when the sky had opened up and unleashed its fury.

Still, she had remained on her knees, her tears mixing with the pouring rain to spill onto Jacob's grave.

A knock sounded on the driver's side window, startling her out of her reflecting. She snatched up her purse, removed the keys from the ignition, and opened the car door.

"I've been worried sick," Owen yelled over the thunder and lightning, white puffs of smoke bursting from his mouth.

He held an umbrella in his hand, which he promptly moved above the open door. "It's freezing out here!"

Jessica climbed out; cold, wet and mentally numb. She handed the keys to Owen and heard more than saw him close the door to the SUV before allowing him to lead her shivering body inside the house.

He guided her up the stairs and into the master bathroom.

The shower came on a moment later, and the warmth of rising steam filled the room.

"Let's get you out of these wet clothes." Owen moved in close and began unbuttoning her soaked blouse.

Jessica stood perfectly still while her husband worked on disrobing her. "Can you get me my pills?"

He hesitated, his fingers on the button of her jeans. "How many have you had today?"

Indignation reared its head. "Do I ask you how many drinks you have a day?"

He stared down at her from his taller height of six feet two. "No. That would mean you actually cared."

Jessica looked away, unable to deal with another ounce of guilt without crumbling under its weight.

"I'm sorry, Jess. I shouldn't have said that. Let's get you into the shower and then I'll grab your pills."

"Thank you," was all she could manage, stepping out of her wet jeans and climbing into the shower.

The hot water felt good on her chilled flesh. She shuddered in relief as warmth seeped into her body, forcing back the cold and relaxing her tense muscles.

"Did you eat today?" Owen called out from the bathroom doorway.

Jessica couldn't remember the last time she'd eaten. Though she had no appetite even now, she knew she needed food in order to take her meds without hallucinating. "No, I didn't."

There was a brief pause and then, "I put you a plate in the microwave after dinner tonight. I'll just warm it up."

She wanted to thank him but couldn't conjure up the energy to do so. The door clicked shut a second later.

Jessica finished her shower, dressed in a warm nightgown, and made her way downstairs on wooden legs.

A plate of meatloaf, mashed potatoes, and green beans sat on the table next to a glass of tea and two small, white pills. Owen was nowhere in sight.

The sounds of the television spilled from the living room as Jessica took a seat and picked up her drink. She grabbed the two pills, tossed them into her mouth and then chased them down with a drink of her tea.

Swallowing the food proved harder than she'd imagined, but she forced down several bites out of necessity.

Owen's handsome face appeared around the wall. "Do you need anything?"

"I'm good. What are you watching?" *He really is handsome,* Jessica thought, taking in his dark, tousled hair and light blue eyes. More guilt assailed her.

He stepped into the dining room, his glass of wine in hand, and took a seat across from her at the table. "Just the local news. It's supposed to rain on into tomorrow."

"I wasn't planning on going out anywhere." She took another bite of her meatloaf.

Owen gazed down into his glass of wine. "You could try painting again. You haven't picked up a paintbrush since before... "

"You can say it, Owen. Since before Jacob died."

He seemed to ignore her jab. "We need to talk about Florida, Jess."

"There's nothing to talk about. I'm not selling this house, and I'm not packing up Jacob's things as if he never existed."

Without looking up from the contents of his glass, Owen asked, "Would you be willing to go if we didn't sell the house?"

"How could we afford to move without selling?"

Owen looked up. "We'll dip into our savings and take out a loan against my retirement if necessary."

Anxiety surfaced at the thought of not having access to Jacob's room…his things. Deep down, Jessica understood that Owen was attempting to help her, knew that moving was the right thing to do. But she couldn't bring herself to agree. "I'll think about it."

"That's all I ask." Owen got to his feet. "I'm going to bed. I'll see you in the morning."

Jessica watched him go in a daze as the effects of her medication began to take hold. She briefly closed her eyes, grateful for the slight numbness the drugs always gave her.

She pushed her plate aside, picked up Owen's half empty glass of wine, and took a sip. The tangy liquid slid down her throat, numbing her even more.

Taking the glass with her, Jessica stood and carried her plate to the kitchen. She scraped off the excess food into the trashcan and loaded the plate into the dishwasher.

After downing the glass of wine, she picked up the bottle sitting on the counter and made her way upstairs to Jacob's room.

The door stood ajar, just as she'd left it the night before. She pushed it open and stepped inside.

As with every other visit to her son's bedroom, the longing to see him curled up in bed overtook her.

She swallowed back her tears, took another drink of wine, and moved to stand in front of Jacob's dresser.

The same dirty shirt he'd worn over three years ago lay draped over the dresser top exactly as it always had. She picked it up and brought it to her nose.

Jacob's scent had long since disappeared, leaving a hole in Jessica's heart to rival the one in her soul.

She glanced around the room, the tears she'd tried to hold back now spilling down her cheeks. Could she really move to Florida and leave Jacob behind?

Turning to replace the small shirt onto the dresser, Jessica caught a glimpse of herself in the mirror. Even in the oversized nightgown, she looked rail thin. She was slowly grieving herself to death and destroying her marriage in the process. If she hadn't already...

Chapter Three

Florida

Three Months Later

Owen glanced in the rearview mirror of the moving truck he'd procured and backed into the drive of their new home in Sparkleberry Hills, Florida.

Jessica hadn't spoken much on the long drive from Chicago, but she'd agreed to come and that was all that mattered to Owen in that moment.

After watching her nearly grieve herself to death for the past three and a half years, Owen was willing to do just about anything to bring her back from the edge. That included moving to a small town in the panhandle of Florida.

Sparkleberry Hills had been the last place Owen wanted to go. He loved Illinois. He'd been born and raised in Chicago, had a great job as a bank manager, and a decent retirement already built up. At thirty-eight years old, Owen had managed to buy a nice home and make some pretty smart investments. Life had been good until the accident that claimed his only son's life.

Not a day went by that Owen didn't think of Jacob. He had grieved the death of his son to the point of almost losing his mind. He'd been forced to hide his grief behind a mask of strength he didn't feel in order to be strong for Jess.

The Jess Owen had married had faded away to a shell of her former self. She'd lost so much weight that her clothes hung on her and dark circles rested beneath her pretty green eyes.

He hoped and prayed he hadn't made a huge mistake in bringing her to Florida. "Am I clear on your side?"

She rolled down her window and stuck her head out to look behind them. "You have about a foot clearance over here. But there's a low-lying limb that might scratch the truck."

Tugging the gear into drive, Owen pulled forward a few feet, turned the wheel a little and backed up once more.

"You're good," Jess called, her head remaining out the window.

Owen stopped the moving truck and switched off the engine. "Let's go have a look."

He waited for Jess to get out before opening his door and climbing down as well.

The pale-green cottage sat under a copse of giant oak trees. Moss hung from their low-hanging branches, gently swaying in the breeze blowing through. Rose bushes grew beneath the two white shuttered windows on the front of the house, giving the place a warm, inviting feeling.

Owen glanced at Jess. "What do you think?"

"It's prettier than the pictures." She never took her gaze from the house as she spoke. "Though it looks kind of small."

"Let's go have a peek. I was told the inside was bigger than it appears from out here."

Jessica nodded, trailing slowly up the driveway that lead to the front porch. She stopped and waited for Owen to unlock the door.

He preceded her inside, flipping on the lights as he went. Though it was just after noon, the shade from the many oak trees made lights a necessity during the day.

The living room walls were a mint green, trimmed in white. The floors boasted of varnished wood that were bare of any rugs.

They moved on into the dining room to find the same matching paint and floors.

"Watch your footing," Owen warned, nodding to the dip at the entrance to the kitchen.

Jessica stepped down into the spacious room, a small gasp escaping her lips.

It was the first positive reaction Owen had seen from her in longer than he could remember. "You like it?"

"It's beautiful." She moved forward, running her fingertips along the red-tiled kitchen counters.

The backsplash had been tiled as well in a black-and-white checkered pattern. The sink, stove, and refrigerator were a deep onyx and the microwave a blood red, same as the counters. The checkered floor tiles set off the rest of the room as did the deep, red rug in the center.

After spending several minutes admiring the kitchen, Owen left Jessica to acquaint herself with the rest of the house while he unloaded the truck.

She eventually wandered out to help him.

"You should go rest," Owen offered, watching her struggle with a box. "The movers will be here shortly with the furniture. They can help me with this stuff."

"Are you sure?"

A moving truck turned onto the street just then. "I'm positive. In fact, there they are now. I'll have them set up the bed first thing so you can relax a bit before dinner."

She set the box down by the back of the truck. "What are we going to do for dinner?"

Owen shrugged. "We'll Google some local establishments and see what pops up. Hopefully, they'll have Chinese."

Attempting a small smile, Jessica nodded and trailed back toward the house.

Chapter Four

Jessica moved through the rooms of her new house, undeniably detached. At any other time, she would have loved the new place, but not without Jacob.

A feeling of anxiety swept through her, sending the room spinning around her. She leaned heavily against the wall and squeezed her eyes shut tightly. She couldn't have a panic attack her first day in the new place...she just couldn't.

"Hello?"

The sound of a woman's voice echoed off the walls of the living room, high-pitched and nasally. "Anyone here?"

Jessica's eyes flew open. She sucked in great gulps of air attempting to rein in her panic. "I'll be right there," she managed to gasp between bouts of dizziness.

"Not a problem. Take your time."

After several more heartbeats of leaning against the wall for support, Jessica managed to survive her attack. But the anxiety she felt inside still remained.

She straightened her shirt, ran a hand through her long, dark hair, and forced one foot in front of the other.

"I hope I didn't disturb you?" a short, plump woman with bleached blonde hair announced with a smile. She held a covered dish in her hands.

Jessica attempted to return her smile but failed miserably. "You didn't."

"I'm Margarette Hawthorn, but my friends call me Marge. I live on the other side of the cul-de-sac, on the right. The one with the fish mailbox."

"I didn't notice a mailbox. Sorry."

Marge appeared uncomfortable. She suddenly thrust the dish she held at Jessica. "I'd heard y'all would be arriving today, so I made you a casserole to welcome you into the neighborhood. I hope you like it."

Surprised by the gesture, Jessica accepted the dish. "Thank you, Marge. I'm Jessica, and my husband's name is Owen. You really didn't have to go through all this trouble."

"Well, it's wonderful to meet you, and it's no trouble at all."

An awkward silence fell.

Marge clasped her hands in front of her and gazed around at the bare walls. "I see they painted since the last time I was here."

"You knew the people who lived here before us?" Jessica trailed off into the kitchen to put the casserole away.

Marge followed. "They were a really nice couple. Had two rambunctious children. Do you and your husband have any kids?"

Jessica's throat closed. She set the dish down onto the countertop and shook her head.

"Oh, that's too bad," Marge continued, obviously not noticing Jessica's distress. "Well, you're still young, I'm sure you'll fill the house with little ones in no time."

Fighting back the tears that threatened, Jessica cleared her throat and turned to face her neighbor. "Thank you again for the casserole, Mrs. Hawthorn. I would offer you a drink, but we haven't unloaded the dishes yet."

"Please, call me Marge," the woman insisted, turning back toward the living room. "I'll get out of your hair. But once you are settled, Benny and I would love to have you over for dinner."

The last thing Jessica wanted was to mingle with the neighbors. She craved nothing more than to be left alone. Regardless, she found herself saying, "That would be nice. Thank you."

Marge nodded and then left, leaving Jessica to wonder what had just happened. She'd never had anyone bring her a casserole in Chicago. Not that she had many friends. She didn't. She'd had fewer still after Jacob's death.

"Who was that?" Owen came through the door, carrying a large box with the word *PICTURES* scrawled across the top.

Jessica pointed toward the far corner of the living room. "You can put that over there. The woman who just left is one of our neighbors. Her name is Marge Hawthorn. She brought us a casserole."

Owen set the box down and straightened. "A casserole? What for?"

Jessica shrugged. "Sort of a house warming gift, I think."

"That was nice of her." Owen wiped the sweat from his forehead with the back of his arm.

It *was* nice, Jessica silently agreed, hoping she hadn't come across as rude to the woman.

Several different men began filing into the house carrying boxes. Jessica stepped aside as Owen lead them all to specific rooms.

"I'm going to have a look around outside," she called out, hoping her husband heard her over the murmuring of voices inside the house.

When no response came, she strode through the open front door and into the yard.

The place really was beautiful to Jessica. She'd never seen trees the size of the ones surrounding the house. They were majestic with their low-lying limbs twisting toward the ground in different shapes.

Jessica appreciated the fact that the house sat at the end of the cul-de-sac, it assured more privacy.

She moved around the yard, her gaze straying to the wooden, two-story house on the left side of the cul-de-sac.

The place appeared to have been empty for some time if the peeling paint and overgrown grass were any indication. One of the downstairs windows was busted and an old, dingy-white curtain hung half askew from its shattered pane.

An icy wind suddenly swept through the yard, sending goosebumps peppering her skin. Jessica rubbed at her arms, her gaze glued to the front of that house. It seemed to call to her, silently beckoning her forward.

She trailed across the lawn, dodging the swaying moss that hung from the oak trees until she reached the adjoining property line.

Another burst of cold air appeared, sweeping through the grass and stirring up the leaves at Jessica's feet. The chilly wind felt out of place on the otherwise warm, summer day.

A strange sensation overtook her in that moment, raising the fine hairs on the back of her neck. Something bad had happened in that house. Jessica wasn't sure how she knew it, she only knew that she did.

She turned to go when movement in the upstairs window caught her eye. She squinted against the glare of sunlight trickling through the trees and peered up at the dirty glass of the window. There, staring back at her, stood a dark-haired boy, wearing what looked to be a striped T-shirt.

He couldn't be more than seven years old, she guessed, attempting to make out his features. *The same age as Jacob had been before…* She couldn't finish the thought.

Jessica lifted a hand, sending him a quick wave, but the boy didn't reciprocate. He continued to stare down at her for long moments before backing from her view altogether.

Chapter Five

Jessica scanned the area surrounding the empty house for a bike or other signs of children at play but came up empty. Aside from the boy she'd seen in the window, no evidence of life existed at the place.

She trekked carefully through the overgrown grass and made her way to the front door to try the knob. Locked. *Surely the child didn't climb through the broken window?*

Chewing on the inside of her mouth, Jessica decided she'd skirt the house and try the back door.

She spun around and nearly ran into a thick, balding man standing directly behind her.

"Jesus!" She stumbled back a step, her hand flying to her chest. "You startled me."

When the man simply stood there watching her with a pair of hawk-like eyes, Jessica inched back another step. "You must be one of my neighbors. I just moved in next door."

"You're trespassing," was his only response.

More than a little uncomfortable under his scrutiny, Jessica fidgeted with the collar of her shirt. "I'm sorry. I had no idea this was private property. I'll just be going then."

Without bothering to move back and allow her to pass, he folded his arms over his thick chest, drawing attention to a greasy food stain on his white T-shirt.

Jessica's heart began to pound. She'd never been so uncomfortable in all her life. He reminded her of a wife-beating psychopath she'd seen in a movie, some years ago.

"Eustis!" a woman called from the red-brick house to their left. "Where are you?"

The man's already ruddy face turned nearly purple with obvious rage. He flicked a glance in the direction the voice had come from and then spun on his heel and marched off.

More than a little anxious to be gone, Jessica hurried across the overgrown lawn, not stopping until she reached the protection of the oak trees in her own front yard.

She peered over her shoulder in time to watch the creepy balding man disappear inside the red-brick house.

* * * *

The rest of the day was spent in a flurry of unloading and unpacking. Yet, no matter how busy Jessica became, she couldn't shake the eerie feeling the creepy neighbor had left her with.

The sound of a door slamming startled her. She glanced up to find Owen watching her with a strange look in his eyes.

"What?" she softly questioned, straightening from her task of emptying a box of dishes.

He shook his head. "Nothing. Just appreciating your natural beauty."

"Is that a subtle way of pointing out that I have no make-up on?" Jess forced a smile to ensure he knew her to be teasing.

Owen grinned in return. "Now that you mention it…"

She cleared her throat. "It's getting late. Perhaps we should get cleaned up and go in search of a place to eat."

"Have you had a chance to taste that casserole?" Owen stepped down into the kitchen and peeled back the foil covering the glass dish. "It looks delicious."

It smelled delicious too, Jessica noticed. She opened a box of plates and handed two of them to Owen. "Grab a spoon from that drawer to your left and dip us up some."

Owen heaped their plates high with the heavenly smelling food and passed one, along with a fork, to Jess. The two of them took a seat on a couple of still-packed boxes and devoured every last drop of Marge's casserole.

"I saw that you met another of our neighbors in front of that old, abandoned house." Owen got to his feet and rinsed his plate in the sink.

Jess followed suit. "I wouldn't go so far as to say we met."

"What do you mean?"

With a shrug, she loaded both their plates into the dishwasher. "He scared the crap out of me and then proceeded to inform me that I was trespassing."

Owen's eyebrows shot up. "Really?"

"Really. I never even got his name. Plus, there were no signs posted or anything. He probably would have had the bloody runs if he'd seen the kid inside the house."

"What kid?"

Thinking about the small face staring down at her from that dirty window, Jessica shook her head. "I don't know. Just some boy I saw in the upstairs window."

Owen brought his hand up and massaged the back of his neck. "Well, hopefully he made it out of there with his hide intact."

"Yeah, maybe so." Rinsing out the empty casserole dish, Jess loaded it into the dishwasher and then stepped up into the dining room. "I'm going to take a shower. I'll make the bed as soon as I get out."

"Sounds good."

Jessica spent the next twenty minutes enjoying her shower, her mind processing everything that had happened since her arrival in Sparkleberry Hills. But nothing stood out as much as that old house sharing the cul-de-sac with her or the little boy staring down at her from that window. He'd reminded her of Jacob.

She frantically scrubbed at her scalp in an effort to push thoughts of Jacob from her mind. Without the medication to dull her senses, the pain of his passing was as fresh as if it had happened yesterday.

Her psychiatrist has begun weaning her off the pills the week after her last visit with Dr. Knox—the day Owen had dropped the mother of all bombs on her...his job transfer.

Jessica had fought Owen at every turn, refusing to leave the home Jacob had lived in since birth. But she'd eventually given in. Deep down, she'd known her husband to be right, she would have never been able to get on with her life as long as she remained in that house.

Practicing the breathing exercises Doctor Knox had taught her, Jessica took slow, calculated breaths through her nose, exhaling in the same calming manner from her mouth. She concentrated on the task of washing her hair until the overwhelming feeling began to pass.

"Save me some hot water," Owen playfully demanded, opening the bathroom door. "I feel like I've wallowed in a cesspool of sweat."

Jess pasted on a small smile, pulled the curtain back, and poked her head out. "I'm almost done."

"Mind if I join you?"

And just like that, the anxiety was back.

If she allowed Owen into that shower with her, he would want sex. Of that, she had no doubt. He was a healthy, thirty-eight-year-old man who hadn't been with his wife in more than three years.

Jessica stared at his handsome face, the hopeful expression in his eyes, and her heart cracked. What was it about intimacy that terrified her so?

Doctor Knox had theorized that intimacy represented fear to Jessica. It required her opening her heart and emotions to another person; something she hadn't been able to do since Jacob's death.

How could she participate in something meant to be pleasurable when her only child lay in a cold, dark grave? "I'm sorry, Owen. I'll be done in just a minute."

Disappointment shone in his eyes, but he didn't argue. He simply closed the door as quietly as he'd opened it.

Chapter Six

Owen stood in the shower, his tears mingling with the water sluicing down his body. He'd lost more than Jacob on that cold, winter's day over three years ago. He'd lost his wife as well.

Jessica thought he didn't feel as deeply about Jacob's death as she did. She couldn't be more wrong. Owen felt his son's absence in his soul.

In truth, it was harder on Owen to hold his feelings inside; to hide them from his wife in order to remain strong for her. If he'd fallen apart outwardly the way he had inside, Jessica would have never survived.

Owen had grieved every single day since Jacob had been taken from him. He grieved still, to the point he felt less than whole. But life didn't stop for loss, pain, and grief. Life continued on, and Owen had no choice but to continue with it. He could never forget Jacob, nor did he want to. But moving to Florida had been the right decision, and one he hadn't taken lightly. He and Jessica would begin their new life and hopefully find some kind of happiness.

She seemed stronger since coming off some of the medications. Though she still had some antianxiety meds for emergencies.

After finishing his shower, Owen switched off the water and stepped out. He dried quickly before pulling on a pair of boxer-briefs and entering the bedroom.

"Jess?"

When no answer came, he padded barefoot down the hall and into the living room to find her standing at a window, staring out.

He switched on the light. "What are you doing?"

"Turn it off," she whispered without moving.

Owen did as she asked and then trailed across the room to stand behind her. "What is it?"

She jerked her chin toward the old, abandoned house. "Do you see him?"

"See who?" Owen leaned in closer to the glass, his gaze scanning the front of the two-story house.

Jessica moved over a few inches to give him some room. "The boy in the window."

Owen squinted against the street light glare and searched every window on the front of that house. "I don't see anyone."

"There!" Jess whispered impatiently. "Top, left window."

Nothing moved that he could see. Not a curtain, a shadow, or a light. "It was probably just a reflection from the street light. Come on, let's go to bed."

Jessica stiffened. "You think I imagined it." It wasn't a question.

"I didn't say that, Jess."

She turned to face him, her eyes gleaming in the light of the moon spilling through the window. "You didn't have to. I can hear it in your voice."

Owen wanted to ask her if she'd taken some of her emergency meds, but he decided against it. It would only anger her even more. "What you hear in my voice is exhaustion. If you think you saw something in that window...then I believe you."

"I didn't see *something*, Owen. I saw *someone*. It looked like the same child I saw earlier today.

Blowing out a patient breath, Owen took hold of her arm and pulled her against his chest. "I'm sorry, hon. I'm just tired. It could be anyone. In fact, it's probably the local hangout spot for the neighborhood kids. They're probably up there right now smoking cigarettes and playing spin the bottle like we did at their age."

Jessica relaxed against him. "I didn't think of that."

"Come on, let's go." Owen kissed the top of her head and led her back toward the hall.

Once in the bedroom, he pulled back the covers and climbed into their king-size bed.

Jess hesitated before joining him.

She rolled toward him, and to his surprise, placed her head on his chest. "I'm sorry I've been so distant. I'm trying, Owen. I really am."

Owen's heart twisted. He understood how difficult it was for Jess to open up to him. She'd remained closed off since Jacob's passing. "I know you are, babe. I just want you to understand that I'm not going anywhere. I love you more than anything."

She lifted her head and met his gaze. "That means a lot. I love you, too. I may not show it very often, but I do."

He cupped her head in his palm and tugged her back down to his chest. "Get some sleep. We have a big day tomorrow."

Chapter Seven

Jessica remained on Owen's chest long after his breathing became even.

With sleep eluding her, she eased to her side of the bed and tossed back the covers.

Taking one last look at her now snoring husband, she inched out of bed and crept quietly from the room.

It didn't surprise her to find herself back in the living room, staring at the old, abandoned house.

Nothing moved in that upstairs window, no matter how long she stood there watching it. Of course, it was almost midnight...the boy would have gone home by then.

Just as she was about to give up her vigil and return to bed, something moved behind the darkened pane.

Jessica pressed her nose to the glass, stunned to find the boy staring back at her from his previous position.

The street light reflected off the pale skin of his face, leaving no doubt that he watched her as she watched him.

What could he be doing up there? And why was no one looking for him? If that were her child, she'd be frantically running up and down the street, calling his name.

She gave up her post, long enough to grab her robe and slippers, and then hurried outside.

The same, cold wind she'd experienced earlier that day, blew through the trees, lifting her hair from her neck.

Jessica paused, her gaze darting around the cul-de-sac before coming to rest on the red brick house. Thankfully, no lights were on inside.

Instead of going to the front of the abandoned house, she skirted to the back and tried the door to find it locked.

She stepped over to the side and tried the window to the right of the door. It slid open effortlessly.

With a rush of adrenaline, Jessica rested her hands on the window sill and heaved herself over. A relieved breath escaped her lungs when her feet touched the floor on the other side.

"Hello?" She could barely see her way around the darkened room—the streetlight coming through the front windows, her only guide. "Little boy?"

As her eyes adjusted enough to her surroundings, she could make out the tiled pattern of the floor. She was in the kitchen.

She carefully moved forward into what appeared to be a den. An old fireplace sat along the west wall, opposite a staircase.

Jessica inched across the room, gripped the banister, and rested her foot on the bottom step. "Hey, kid?"

Silence.

She glanced behind her, noting the closed, front door before stepping fully onto the stairs. The wood creaked beneath her weight, echoing off the walls of the empty house and sending her stomach into a somersault.

Taking a calming breath, Jess held tightly to the banister and slowly climbed the stairs. "I'm coming up."

After reaching the top, she turned left, stopping outside the room where she'd seen the child.

She gripped the knob and slowly turned it. The door squeaked open with the slightest push. Jessica followed, stepping into the room to find it empty.

Her gaze swept the area, coming to land on what appeared to be a closet. She trailed over to the closed door and tugged it open. Empty as well.

Where could he have gone?

Closing the closet door, Jess turned and bit back a gasp. There, staring out that window, stood the small boy in the striped T-shirt.

She noticed his jeans were too short, and he wore no shoes. "Hi there."

He remained still, as if he hadn't heard her. She wondered if perhaps he couldn't hear. "Little boy?"

Moving closer, she lifted her hand to touch his shoulder, only to jerk it back with the sound of heavy footballs coming up the stairs.

Jess spun to face the door in time to watch the beefy, balding neighbor storm into the room.

"You better have a damn good reason for being in here," he growled, barreling toward her.

Jessica stumbled back a step, her hands out in front of her. "I was just checking on the boy. It's after midnight, and —"

"What boy?"

She gestured behind her. "I saw him in the window. I —"

"I don't know what sort of game you think you're playing, but I'm calling the police."

"Game?" Jess glanced behind her to find the boy not there. Her gaze scanned the room in disbelief, anxiety mingling with panic. "He was just here!"

The irate man grabbed her by the arm and yanked her forward, his breath reeking of alcohol. "You're going to jail for breaking and entering."

He continued to speak, but Jess was no longer listening. The boy she'd seen standing at the window had disappeared as if he'd never been there.

Was she losing her mind? Had she finally snapped under the grief of losing Jacob and had now become delusional? She wasn't sure anymore.

Jess brought her attention back to the snarling man in front of her. "Please...I'm sorry. I thought I saw a child standing in that window. I would have never come up here, otherwise."

"Eustice?" a meek, feminine voice called, coming up the stairs. "Is everything alright?"

A woman that looked to be in her early fifties stepped into the room, wearing a floral print robe and slippers. Her once brown hair was peppered with gray and stood on end as if she'd just rolled out of bed. "My goodness, what is this?"

Jessica met the woman's gaze. "I'm sorry, ma'am. I didn't mean to cause all this fuss. It was just a misunderstanding is all."

The woman's eyes appeared nervous. "You must be the new neighbor."

"I am. My name's Jessica. I truly didn't mean for this to happen."

"We're the Martins. I'm Geraldine, and that's my husband, Eustice. Folks around here call me Gerri."

Jessica attempted to pull free of Eustice's hold. "We only just arrived today. I would never have come up here had it not been for the child I saw."

Gerri glanced around the room. "There's a child up here?"

"Of course there's not," Eustice shot back, tightening his hold on Jessica's arm. "She was up here nosing around after I told her earlier that she was trespassing."

"Jessica?" Owen yelled from downstairs, sending relief pouring through her.

Eustice held onto her a moment longer, before releasing her now bruised arm.

Jess rubbed at her tender skin. "I'm up here, Owen!"

Giving Eustice a wide berth, Jess inched around him, stopping next to Gerri to offer her an apologetic smile. "Again, I'm sorry."

Gerri nodded nervously, her gaze flicking to Eustice.

Owen's footsteps could be heard jogging up the stairs. He came to a sudden stop at the door to the room. "What's going on up here?"

Jess hurried to her husband's side. "Just a misunderstanding. Come on, let's go."

"There was no misunderstanding," Eustice spat. "Your wife was nosing around on private property. I've already warned her about trespassing. She's lucky I don't call the police. Next time, I won't be so nice."

Owen took her by the hand and tugged her behind him. "It won't happen again. You have my word."

Jess peered around Owen in time to see Gerri lower her head as Eustice ambled over to her side. It became more than obvious that his wife feared him.

Eustice spat on the floor before wiping his mouth with the back of his hand. "See that it don't."

His speech pattern told Jess that he lacked education as much as he lacked people skills.

Owen turned without another word and guided Jess down the stairs. He waited until they reached the safety of their own bedroom before speaking. "What in God's name were you thinking?"

Jess moved to the other side of the bed and removed her robe. "I told you, there was a boy in that house."

"And you just took it upon yourself to run over there in the middle of the night without letting me know? What if something had happened to you?"

"What if something had happened to *him*?" she shot back. "Does no one care that there was a young child in that abandoned house at this time of night? And how did you know I was over there?"

Owen sighed and ran a hand down his face. "The front door to that house was standing open. Where was the child? I didn't see anyone when I got there."

Jessica had no answer for him. "I don't know. He was gone by the time I arrived."

"Gone," Owen repeated in a wooden voice.

Pulling back the covers, Jess took off her slippers and climbed in bed. "Yes, gone. Can we please talk about this another time? I just want to go to sleep."

Owen stared at her for a moment longer, before giving her a curt nod. "Fine. But don't ever do that to me again. You scared the shit out of me."

"I won't."

"Promise me, Jess. My heart can't take more of what you put me through tonight. When I woke and found you gone..."

Jessica looked away, unable to take the concern swimming in his eyes. "I promise."

Owen removed his own robe and got into bed next to her. His arm came around her, his lips brushing the side of her face. "I love you."

"Love you, too," she whispered, sliding deeper under the covers and rolling to her side away from him.

Though her eyes slid closed on command, her mind refused to shut down. It became filled with images of a dark-haired boy wearing a striped T-shirt and too small jeans.

Chapter Eight

Jessica pushed her cart through the local grocery store, ignoring the curious looks being tossed her way.

Owen had started his new job earlier that week, leaving Jess alone during the day to finish unpacking and decorate their humble abode.

The first thing on her agenda had been to put some food in the house. She'd already grown tired of carry out.

"Jessica!"

Jess looked up from her perusal of the cold food section to find Mrs. Hawthorn standing next to her. "Hi, Marge."

The short, plump blonde studied the items in Jessica's cart. "That's a lot of carbs. I'd be careful if I were you. You'll end up a diabetic like me."

Unsure of how to respond, Jess turned and plucked up a very expensive gallon of milk. "Is this the only grocery store in town?"

Marge nodded. "There's one in Morhaven, but that's about twenty miles from here."

"That explains why the prices are so high." Jess placed the milk in her cart. "They have no competition."

Marge picked up a pack of cheese. "You got that right."

A thought occurred to Jess. She snagged a bag of shredded cheese, pretending to read the label. "What do you know about the people in the red brick house across the street from yours?"

"The Martins?" Marge's voice took on a gossiping tone. "I know more than I want to. Of course, the entire neighborhood knows their business. Especially when Eustice is drinking. Which is pretty much every day."

"Does he mistreat his wife?"

Marge's voice lowered to a whisper as if she feared being overheard. "He beats on her. Why do you ask? Did you see something?"

Careful not to divulge too much, Jess whispered back, "No, but I could hear him yelling at her."

Marge stepped in closer. "Not that I know this for a fact, mind you, but rumor has it that Gerri couldn't have children due to some female issues, and Eustice blamed her for it. Which, in my opinion, is the reason he puts his hands on her."

Now that she had Marge talking, Jess decided to steer the conversation in a different direction. "So, the Martin's own that old abandoned house next door?"

"They do. Although, I can't imagine why. They bought it about thirteen years ago after that little Dayton boy came up missing."

A strange sensation poured through Jess. "I hadn't heard about that."

"He lived in that house next door to you."

Placing the shredded cheese back onto the shelf, Jess pretended to search for a different kind. "What happened to his parents?"

"The place ended up in foreclosure with the Dayton's spending all their time and resources searching for the child. The Martins bought it after the bank forced the Daytons out."

Jessica's heart went out to the Daytons. She knew exactly how hard it must have been for them to leave the home their son had lived in. She met Marge's gaze. "I wonder why the Martins don't rent it out or sell it?"

Marge shrugged. "Eustice claims that it would take too much money to fix it up enough to sell or rent. Says that once he retires, he'll sink some cash into it and unload it then."

Dropping the cheese into her cart, Jessica forced a smile. "Well, I'd better be going. I have a few more errands to run on my way home. It was nice chatting with you, Marge."

"You too, my dear."

Jess paid for her groceries, loaded them into her small SUV, and drove straight home. She hated lying to Marge about having errands to run, but she'd done what she needed to do to prevent an hour-long gossip-fest from taking place.

Once the groceries were put away, Jess trailed off into the spare room they'd turned into an office and booted up her laptop. It came alive with a hum, going through the designated prompts until the sign on screen appeared.

She entered the passcode, tapping her foot beneath the desk while she waited patiently for the search engine to load. She then typed in: *Missing Florida boy/Dayton.*

Several results popped up onto the screen. Everything from *Missing-Seven-year-old Sparkleberry Hills child,* to *Suspicion surrounding Terry Dayton's disappearance.*

His name was Terry, Jess thought, clicking on one of the articles, only to recoil when they boy's picture came into view. Staring back at her from the screen of her computer was the very boy she'd seen in the window of the house next door. The same house he'd lived in when he'd disappeared.

She covered her mouth with a trembling hand, unable to look away from the small boy's face.

His long dark hair appeared unkept, framing his thin face and resting just above his large, green eyes — eyes that held mischief, and something else she couldn't name. *Sadness?*

Her gaze traveled down to the same striped T-shirt he'd had on the day she and Owen had moved in.

She forced her attention to the article below Terry's image. *Seven-year-old Terry Dayton went missing from his home on January tenth.*

Jessica noticed the date in the article. Terry had been missing for thirteen years, just as Marge had said.

She continued to read. *Terry's parents, Jasper and Melanie Dayton have offered a fifty-thousand-dollar reward for any information leading to the whereabouts of their son. Suspicion surrounding his disappearance is being investigated, though no charges have been filed at this time.*

With her heart pounding out of control, and her pulse thumping in her temples, Jessica finished reading the article before moving on to another. And on it went. She wasn't sure how long she sat there soaking up everything she could on the missing boy when the sound of a car door came from the drive.

Jess glanced at the corner of the computer screen in shock. She'd been sitting there reading non-stop for the past three hours.

"I'm home," Owen announced as he came through the front door. "Jess?"

Jessica closed the lid to the laptop, not wanting to reveal what she'd been reading. If Owen had any idea that she thought the boy she'd seen in that upstairs window was the missing child from thirteen years ago, he would think her crazy. Truth be told, she'd wondered the same thing herself.

Chapter Nine

Owen pulled on his running shoes, deciding to go for a jog while Jessica made dinner. He'd changed from his suit to a pair of gym shorts and a white tank top. "I'll be back shortly."

Jessica scrambled around the kitchen with more energy than she'd displayed in years. "Burgers okay with you?"

"That's fine," he assured her, getting to his feet. He stood next to the dining room table, watching her buzz about in the kitchen. "How are you feeling?"

She slowed her steps but didn't look back at him. "I'm good. Why do you ask?"

Afraid to jinx her energetic mood, Owen ambled toward the front door and called out, "No reason. See you soon."

Once outside, he briskly strode toward the street. Several folks from the neighborhood were bustling about. Some mowing their lawns, while others dragged trashcans to the curbside. Kids rode their bikes, laughing and glancing over their shoulders to taunt the slower ones behind them.

Owen lifted a hand to return the many waves sent his way and took off in a jog.

In the brief time that he and Jess had been in Sparkleberry Hills, Owen had found it calming, if not downright soothing. He'd never realized that leaving the madness of the big city would bring him such peace. But that is exactly what had happened. He actually felt...peace.

Jess, on the other hand, seemed keyed up, more nervous than usual. Owen wasn't sure if that was a good thing or not, but he'd like to think it was.

He'd almost made it to the end of the street, when a tall, blond man sitting on his porch, stood to watch him jog past.

Owen waved, expecting the guy to reciprocate. The man just stood there, his eyes squinting in an aggressive manner.

Okay then, Owen thought, averting his gaze. Apparently not everyone in the neighborhood was friendly.

Owen had run for a good twenty minutes when he decided to turn back and head home. Jessica would surely have dinner ready and she wouldn't eat without him.

Wiping the sweat from his eyes, he turned onto Meadowbrook Circle, intentionally avoiding the sour gaze of the tall, blond still standing on his porch.

A distressed cry reached Owen's ears. He slowed his steps, scanning the rows of houses on either side of the street.

The sound came again, louder this time.

Owen picked up his pace, realizing the cry came from the red brick house up on his right.

It surprised him to see the surrounding neighbors that were once outside, scurry up their driveways to return indoors.

He left the street, jogging across the of the red brick house. "Mrs. Martin?"

No answer.

Owen sailed onto the porch and rapped on the door. "Mrs. Martin? It's your neighbor, Owen Nobles."

The door swung open and Eustice stepped out. "What do you want?"

"I heard someone cry out." Owen attempted to see inside the house, but the balding man stood in the way. "Is everything okay?"

Eustice crossed his arms over his beefy chest. "Everything is fine. Now be on your way."

Owen wasn't about to leave without making sure that Mrs. Martin wasn't injured. "I'll be on my way when I speak to your wife."

The neighbor's eyes narrowed. "What happens on my property is none of your business. Now, I suggest you get off my lawn before I run you off." Eustice touched the pocket of his jeans for emphasis.

The bulge resting there left little doubt in Owen's mind that his neighbor carried a gun.

Bringing his hands up in front of him, Owen slowly backed away. "I'm going."

Without turning his back on the insane man, Owen carefully made his way home and immediately went for his cell phone.

Jessica entered the dining room, wiping her hands on a dish towel. "You're back." Her gaze fell on the cellphone in his hands. "What are you doing?"

"I'm calling the police."

Alarm registered in her eyes. "The police? What for?"

Owen held up a hand for silence after dialing 911. He brought the phone to his ear and waited patiently for the dispatcher to go through her spiel. *"911-what is your emergency?"*

"I believe my neighbor is hurting his wife."

Jessica's gasp wasn't lost on Owen.

"What is the address of the dispute?" The sounds of typing could be heard in the background.

Owen spouted off the address before answering the rest of her questions.

Once the dispatcher had the pertinent information, she demanded he stay on the line with her until the officers arrived.

Her face pale and drawn, Jess took a seat next to him at the dining table and fidgeted with her hands.

More than ten minutes ticked by before the sound of sirens could be heard coming up the street. Owen informed the dispatcher of the officers' arrival and then disconnected the call.

He met Jess's worried gaze. "I hope I didn't just make things worse for Mrs. Martin."

"How could you make it worse?"

"Trust me. It can always get worse."

Shouting suddenly ricocheted off the trees out front, sending both Owen and Jess surging to their feet. They scrambled to the front window.

Eustice stood on his porch, his hand waving angrily in front of him as he faced off with the police officers. He abruptly turned, jerked his front door open and Mrs. Martin stepped outside.

Even from a distance, Owen could see the bruising on her face.

Putting a finger to his lips for quiet, Owen eased his window up in hopes of hearing the conversation. Alas, Mrs. Martin's voice was too soft to make out her words.

The police stayed for a few minutes more, and then trekked their way across the yard of the abandoned house to Owen's place.

Owen promptly let them in.

"Are you the one who called in the complaint?" a tall, thin officer asked.

Owen nodded. "I am."

The officer reached into his shirt pocket and pulled a small notepad free. "Your name, sir?"

"Owen Nobles, and this is my wife, Jessica."

Jessica cleared her throat and jerked her chin toward the window. "Is Mr. Martin going to jail?"

The officer shook his head. "We have nothing to charge him with."

"Nothing to charge him with?" Jess blurted. "But he was obviously beating on his wife."

The tall, thin officer met her gaze. "This isn't the first time we've been called out to the Martins' on domestic abuse allegations. But the wife always comes to his defense."

Owen's eyebrows shot up. "How can she defend him? It's obvious he beats her. Hell, I could see the bruises from over here."

"She claims that she fell down the stairs of the house next door," the officer answered.

Owen's hands went to his hips. "She wasn't in the house next door. The cries I heard were coming from inside the brick home."

"I understand, Mr. Nobles. Unfortunately, if the wife refuses to press charges, there's nothing we can do."

Jess threw up a hand in obvious disbelief. "And if he kills her? Then what?"

"Then we have a case." The officer finished jotting down something on the notepad, flipped it closed and returned it to his shirt pocket.

"Look, folks, I know you mean well, and we appreciate you attempting to help. But we see this sort of thing more often than not. The abused are either too afraid to make a report, or they have some deep rooted need to be controlled."

Jess opened her mouth to argue, but Owen sent her a look he hoped she would read. She did.

He extended his hand to the officer. "Thank you for responding."

"That's what we're here for."

Chapter Ten

Jessica watched the officers stride back to their squad car and leave without a backward glance. "I can't believe they're not going to do anything."

Owen closed the door. "You heard them. Their hands are tied. If Mrs. Martin refuses to press charges, there's nothing they can do."

"But you saw the marks on her face." Jess moved to the window to find Eustice standing on his front porch staring back at her.

She quickly backed away, a feeling of unease following her into the kitchen. "Dinner's getting cold."

Owen stepped up behind her and wrapped her in his arms. "It smells delicious. Listen, Jess, I want you to stay away from the house next door. I don't want you anywhere near Eustice Martin when I'm not here."

Jess merely nodded. She picked up a plate that held a burger and homemade french fries and offered it to her husband.

Kissing the top of her head, Owen accepted the plate and took it into the dining room.

Jessica quickly joined him.

The two of them ate in silence, each one lost in his or her own thoughts. Jess couldn't help but think about the articles she'd read before Owen's arrival home.

What suspicions had surrounded the investigation? she silently questioned, taking a bite of her burger. *And who were they suspicious of?*

She wondered if Eustice Martin had anything to do with it. Strange that he'd bought that house shortly after its foreclosure.

Owen paused with his burger half way to his mouth. "Don't worry about the Martins,

Jess. As long as you steer clear of their property, everything will be alright."

Jessica nodded in an attempt to reassure Owen that she would be fine. When, in truth, she felt anything but. Her gut told her that Eustice had more than likely been trouble to the people who'd lived in that two-story house, and she wouldn't be surprised if he had something to do with Terry's disappearance.

Owen reached out and laid his palm over the back of Jessica's hand. "Are you sure you're okay?"

With a small smile, Jess put down her burger and wiped her mouth. "I'm sure. Let's finish eating and watch a movie together."

His eyes lit up with joy, sending a pang of guilt sliding through her gut. She'd neglected him—neglected his needs for the past three years, yet he'd always been there for her.

They finished their meal in silence, cleaned up their mess, and got ready for bed.

Owen turned on the television in the bedroom. "What do you want to watch?"

"It doesn't matter." And it didn't. TV didn't interest her in the least. Seeing Owen smile was her only goal tonight. "You pick something."

He pulled her head down to his chest as he'd recently done and flipped through the channels. It wasn't long until the room filled with the soft sounds of his snores.

Jess switched off the television and quietly slid from the bed. Sleep would surely allude her this night, her mind becoming a jumble of scattered thoughts and images of the day's events.

She crept to her office and flipped on the light. Her painting supplies sat in the corner, resting against the wall. She hadn't painted in years.

Setting up the easel, Jess began readying her paints along with a fresh canvas. She wanted to create Jacob, smiling and playing in the sun.

It took her a good minute to gather enough strength to mix her paints. It wouldn't be easy to capture the image of a smiling Jacob, not with her last memory of him lying in that coffin.

Swallowing hard, Jess steadied her hand and started with the backdrop. It wasn't long before she became lost in the feel of the brush moving over the canvas.

* * * *

"Jess?" Owen's voice penetrated her sleep fogged brain. "What are you doing in here? It's three in the morning."

Blinking to clear her vision, Jess met her husband's worried gaze. "I couldn't sleep, so I thought I'd come in here and paint."

She shifted her attention to the canvas, the brush she held in her fingers falling softly to the floor at her feet.

Owen rushed into the room. "Are you okay?"

Jess couldn't answer. Her gaze remained locked on the image before her — the image of a boy, lying in a grave. Though, she couldn't see his face for the long, dark hair, covering his eyes, she would recognize that striped T-shirt, anywhere.

She cleared her throat, jumping to her feet and blocking Owen's view of the painting. "It's not finished yet."

Owen came to a stop, his gaze searching her own. "You look like you've seen a ghost."

He had no idea how accurate his assessment was. Jessica blanked her expression. "I must have fallen asleep in here. I'm sorry for worrying you. Go back to bed, I'll be there shortly."

Owen's shoulders visibly relaxed. "It's good to see you taking an interest in painting again."

Jess sent him a reassuring smile. "It actually felt pretty good."

He turned to go. "Don't stay up too much longer. You look exhausted."

Jessica waited for him to disappear around the corner before moving back in front of the image she had no memory of painting.

Her hand slowly lifted toward the little boy's hidden face, but she let it fall away.

She would need to get rid of the painting before Owen saw it. He already worried about her sanity, and if he had any idea that she'd blacked out and painted the missing Dayton boy, buried beneath the ground, he would think she'd lost her mind. At this point, Jessica was beginning to question that very thing.

Snatching up the painting, she hurried across the room and placed it in the back of the closet.

Chapter Eleven

Jessica spent the next few days reading everything she could find on the internet about the missing Dayton boy.

In all the articles she'd found, one man's name continued to appear—a reporter named Steven Ruckle.

She backed out of the current screen she'd landed on and typed in the reporter's name. Steven Ruckle no longer worked as a reporter for the local newspaper. He'd moved on to an editor's position at a much larger publishing house.

Jess wrote down the phone number that appeared on the screen and reached for her cell.

What am I going to say? Hi, my name is Jessica Nobles and I saw the missing boy from the house next door? They will lock me up for sure.

Taking a steadying breath, Jess dialed the number.

"Harrington Post," a female voice announced, picking up on the third ring.

Jess wanted to hang up. Instead, she said, "May I speak with Steven Ruckle?"

"He's not in his office at the moment, but I can take a message if you'd like?"

Jessica gave the woman her name and number. "Thank you for your time."

"Not a problem." The woman disconnected the call.

Dropping her cellphone into her skirt pocket, Jessica ambled toward the kitchen for a drink of water. The cell vibrated against her hip before she finished filling her glass.

She set her drink on the counter, checked the ID screen of her phone and pressed the green key. "Hello?"

"This is Steven Ruckle. I had a message to give you a call."

Jessica's heart began to race. "Hi, Mr. Ruckle. My name is Jessica Nobles. My husband and I bought the house next door to the old Dayton place. I wondered if I could ask you a few questions about what happened there?"

A pause ensued. "What would you like to know?"

Jessica grew more nervous by the second. "The articles I read online stated that there was some suspicion surrounding the Dayton boy's disappearance, yet it doesn't give specifics about those suspicions."

Steven sighed through the line. "I'm really not the person to question about this, Mrs. Nobles. Perhaps you should speak to the detective assigned to Terry's case."

Odd that he'd used the child's first name, Jess thought. That told her one thing for certain, that he'd been closer to the Dayton case than he wanted to let on.

"Okay, Mr. Ruckle. I apologize for wasting your time."

She moved to end the call when his next words stopped her. "Is the Dayton house still empty?"

"Yes. It's owned by a Mr. Martin. He's the man—"

"Unfortunately, I know exactly who Mr. Martin is. Have you met him yet?"

Jessica moved to the dining room to take a seat at the table. "I had the displeasure my first day in the new neighborhood. I'd gone over to the Dayton house to check on a child I'd seen in the upstairs window when I was nearly accosted by Mr. Martin."

"Accosted?"

"He accused me of trespassing, threatened to call the police on me. But it wasn't until later that night that things got physical."

"What do you mean, things got physical?"

Jess proceeded to tell him about the child she'd seen in the upstairs window, her illegal entry into the house, and Mr. Martin's unexpected appearance.

"Can we meet in person?" Steven suddenly asked, catching her off guard.

Glancing at the clock on the wall, Jessica calculated how much time she had before Owen would be home from work. "Sure. Where would you like to meet?"

"I haven't had lunch yet. How about Happy's Bar and Grill on Highway 2, in say, twenty minutes?"

Jessica fought back the anxiety that assailed her. She was sneaking around behind Owen's back. Though, he left her no choice. If he knew that she was digging around into the missing Dayton boy's case, he'd cart her off to the nearest psychiatrist. "I'll be there."

Ending the call, Jess ran into the bedroom and grabbed her purse. She fished around inside until her fingers touched on the bottle of antianxiety pills she had for emergencies.

She twisted off the lid and popped one into her mouth before hurrying back to the kitchen and downing the glass of water she'd poured.

Normally, Jess would have bypassed the medication unless things began to feel out of control, but today was important. She would be meeting with the reporter on the old Terry Dayton case. She needed to be calm and not come across as the lunatic she no doubt was.

* * * *

Jessica pulled up in front of Happy's Bar and Grill and switched off the engine. The place appeared crowded from what she could see through the row of windows across the front.

"What am I doing here?" Jess muttered aloud, her fingers moving back to the keys still in the ignition.

Her cellphone vibrated from the console, startling her out of fleeing.

She picked it up and took in a number she didn't recognize. Pressing the send key, she brought it to her ear. "Hello?"

"Mrs. Nobles?"

"Yes."

"This is Steven Ruckle. I got here a little early. I'm in the back-left corner in a booth."

"I'm here as well. I'll be right in."

With little choice but to leave or go inside and get the answers she sought, Jessica opened the door and climbed out.

She hoisted her purse onto her shoulder, entered the establishment, and made her way to the back.

A man sat in a booth on the far-left side of the room holding a menu in his hands. He looked up as she approached, a smile on his face. "Mrs. Nobles?"

Jessica nodded and took a seat across from him. She set her purse against the wall next to her and extended her hand across the table.

"Steven Ruckle," he informed her, accepting her palm.

Jess noticed several things at once. His light brown hair appeared windblown, and laugh lines rested at the corners of his eyes. Her gaze lowered to his smile to take in his even, white teeth. "It's nice to meet you."

Releasing her hand, Steven nodded toward the menu lying in front of her. "I hope you're hungry."

She wasn't, but she picked up the menu anyway. She'd rather have something in front of her to fidget with besides her hands. "I could eat."

The waitress arrived to take their orders before bustling off and returning with their drinks.

Jessica stirred some artificial sweetener into her glass of tea, surprised to find Steven had ordered coffee. "I read that you're in editing now."

He took a sip of his coffee. "For nearly nine years. How about you, what do you do?"

"I worked in the school system for quite some time. I haven't gotten a job since moving here. Though, I've only been here for a few weeks."

Steven set down his coffee cup. "I've always been a get-right-to-the-point kind of guy, so that's exactly what I'm going to do. When you said that you saw a child in the Dayton house, what exactly did you see?"

Jessica wondered about his blunt question but decided to be as honest as she could without appearing to be insane. "I saw a young boy in the upstairs window. When I got up there, he was already gone."

"I see. Can you describe him to me?"

"Not really. He had long, dark hair and wore a striped T-shirt. Why?"

Steven leaned back in his seat. "When I was covering that case, there was a woman who lived across the street claiming to have seen something similar. I spoke with her briefly. But when I went back to question her further, she'd moved without leaving a forwarding address."

Jessica's stomach flipped. "Do you think she had something to do with Terry's disappearance?"

"I doubt it. She and her kids were out of town on vacation when he came up missing."

Letting that information soak in, Jessica asked, "What happened to the child's parents?"

"After losing their home, and no doubt their minds, they had no choice but to move. Last I heard, they were living in Morhaven, which is about a twenty-minute drive from here."

Jess nodded, unable to get the image of that painting out of her mind of that boy with the tousled hair, striped shirt...and that grave. "Do you think Eustice Martin had anything to do with Terry's disappearance?"

Steven shrugged. "I think he was involved in something, I'm just not sure what. Why do you ask?"

"I know what I saw in that upstairs window, Mr. Ruckle. What if Terry is still alive and Eustice Martin is holding him somehow?"

Steven's eyebrows shot up. "You do realize the police went over every inch of that place. There's no way Terry Dayton could have been in that house."

"Not at that time, but the Martins bought the house shortly after the Daytons moved. It's been sitting empty for nearly thirteen years.

"Mrs. Nobles...Terry would be twenty years old today. Do you really think old man Martin could keep him locked up in that house? And even if it were possible, the boy you saw was a child, right? It's just not feasible."

Realizing she sounded like a headcase, Jessica grabbed her purse and moved to stand. "I'm sorry I wasted your time."

Steven reached across the table and closed his fingers around her wrist. "Please, sit back down. I didn't mean to be so insensitive."

"I'm not crazy," Jessica whispered, her voice sounding weak to her own ears.

"I never said you were. I asked you here because of what you told me on the phone."

Relaxing the grip she had on her purse, Jessica searched his face. "What do you mean?"

"I do believe the child you saw in that window was Terry Dayton."

"But, you just said—"

"I know what I said. If Terry were still alive, he'd now be a man. But I don't believe he's alive."

"You mean..."

"I believe something happened to him in that house, Mrs. Nobles. I also think he's haunting the place."

Chapter Twelve

Jessica drove home more than a little shaken from her meeting with Steven.

He'd told her all about Mrs. Weaver, the woman who'd lived next door to the Hawthorns.

Jess had learned about Sandy Weaver's sightings of Terry Dayton months after his disappearance, and how she'd packed up and left in the middle of the night shortly thereafter.

Steven had also divulged more insight into the Weaver woman and why her statements hadn't been taken seriously by the police. Sandy Weaver had claimed to be psychic.

Jessica didn't believe in psychics any more than she believed in ghosts, yet the evidence of the supernatural had appeared in that window in the form of Terry Dayton.

Pulling into her drive, Jess noticed Owen's car parked in the garage. She glanced at her watch, surprised to find that she'd been gone for two hours. Still, Owen was home earlier than usual.

She exited the car and trailed up the walk to the front of the house.

The door opened before she reached it. Owen stood there, his tie hanging askew, and his brown hair standing on end as if he'd ran his fingers through it several times. "I've been worried sick."

Jessica avoided his gaze and slipped past him through the open doorway. "You're home early."

"I wanted to surprise you. Why haven't you been answering your phone?"

She'd left her cell in the SUV during her meeting with Steven. "I'm sorry. The ringer must have been off."

Owen followed her into the kitchen, stopping directly behind her as she opened the fridge in search of a drink. "I'm just glad you're okay. Where'd you go?"

Jessica couldn't tell him of her meeting with Ruckle. She grabbed a diet soda and turned to face her husband. "I had lunch in town and then drove around for a while after. It was a nice day, so I decided to do some sightseeing."

Owen's eyes narrowed as if trying to decide if she were being honest with him. "Did you enjoy yourself?"

Nodding, Jess stepped around him and strode toward the bedroom. She didn't blame Owen for questioning her. She had, after all, been suicidal not too long ago.

She changed out of her clothes and donned a soft, pink robe before slipping her feet into a pair of slippers. "Are you hungry?"

Owen answered her from the living room area. "Not really. Would you like to go to an early movie in town?"

The last thing she wanted was to see a movie, especially not with everything she'd recently learned still spinning through her head. Instead, she said, "Sure. Let me put my clothes back on."

Peeling off the robe and slippers, Jessica redressed and met Owen in the living room. "Any idea what you want to see?"

"A comedy if they have one playing."

It didn't matter what they watched to Jess. If it made Owen happy, she would sit through ten documentaries. "Let's go."

* * * *

The two of them stood in a long line at the small movie theater in town. Apparently, they weren't the only ones looking for a brief escape from reality.

The feeling of being watched suddenly slid down Jessica's spine. She shivered from the sensation, her gaze scanning the lobby of the movie theater to find people laughing, talking, and ordering popcorn. But no one seemed to notice her.

She shook off the suspicion and reached for Owen's hand.

"I'm glad we decided to do this," he informed her, giving her palm a gentle squeeze.

Jessica titled her head back to look into his blue eyes. "Me too."

With their tickets in hand, the two of them strode through the lobby, taking a left toward the designated theater room. Yet, the feeling of being watched only intensified.

Jess moved in closer to Owen's side, glancing over her shoulder as they entered the darkened auditorium.

Owen led her to a seat on the seventh row and lowered himself into the chair next to her. "What is it?"

She shook her head. Really, what could she tell him? I feel like I'm being watched? He would think her crazier than he already did. "Nothing. I just thought I saw Mrs. Hawthorn," she easily lied.

The movie previews abruptly started, saving Jessica from further explanation. She sat through the first ten minutes, pretending to watch alongside Owen before the comedy they'd came to see finally began.

Owen's hearty chuckles warmed Jessica's heart. She would give anything to be able to laugh again, to find humor in life the way she'd done before Jacob's passing.

A chill passed along the back of her neck as if a winter wind had blown through the room. It reminded her of the icy breeze she'd felt outside the Dayton house the night they'd moved in next door.

She shivered, hugging her arms tightly around her waist, and slowly twisted her head to look behind her. There, seated in the back of the theater was Terry Dayton.

Jessica quickly faced forward, her heart racing to the point it became painful.

He suddenly walked past, taking the ramp down toward the exit.

She wasn't about to follow—couldn't if she'd wanted to. Her legs shook so bad, she was afraid to stand, yet she found herself doing exactly that.

"I'll be right back," she whispered in Owen's ear on her way out of the aisle.

He nodded, attempting to see around her as she stepped over his booted feet.

What am I doing? she silently chanted, hurrying down the ramp she'd seen the Dayton boy take.

She emerged in the hall in time to see him disappear into the men's restroom.

Jess stopped outside the door, glancing up and down the hall to be sure she wasn't seen, and then slipped quietly inside. "Terry?"

A giant of a man stepped from a stall, his hands on the zipper of his pants. "Uh, lady, this is the men's room."

Embarrassed beyond words, Jess said the first thing that came to mind. "Did you see a little boy with dark hair come in here? He was wearing jeans and a striped T-shirt."

The man shook his head and moved to the sink to wash his hands. "No one's in here but me."

"But I saw him come in here less than a minute ago," she argued, her gaze searching under the doors of the stalls.

"As you can see, he's not here." The man moved away from the sink, turned around, and began pushing all the stall doors open. "Empty."

Jessica muttered her thanks and hurried from the restroom. She staggered to the side once she reached the hallway to lean heavily against the wall. After more than three years since her son's death, Jessica had finally lost her grip on reality.

Chapter Thirteen

Jessica kissed Owen goodbye as he headed out the door to work the following morning.

She'd spent several hours the night before on the internet, searching for the psychic who'd lived next door to the Hawthorns — the only other person to see Terry Dayton after his disappearance...Sandy Weaver.

Listening for the sound of Owen's car to leave the drive, Jessica pulled the woman's number from the pocket of her robe and went in search of her cellphone.

It took several attempts to dial Sandy's number before the call finally connected.

"Hello?" a nervous sounding voice answered.

Jess could relate. She was as nervous as a cat covering shit. "Mrs. Weaver?"

Silence.

"Mrs. Weaver? My name is Jessica Nobles. I was hoping to have a minute of your time to talk to you about—"

"I know what you want," Sandy Weaver blurted, cutting off the rest of Jessica's words.

Jess cleared her throat. "I need your help."

"Leave me be, Mrs. Nobles. There's nothing I can do to help you."

"But—" The line went dead.

Jessica pulled her phone away from her ear and stared at the empty screen for several moments before redialing Sandy's number. It went to voicemail.

"Dammit." Pushing the end key on her cell, Jess strode into her office on wooden legs. If Sandy Weaver refused to speak with her by phone, she'd simply visit her in person.

She booted up her laptop and returned to the screen she'd been on the night before.

Laying the scrap of paper on her desk, she jotted down Sandy's address and then inserted it into the map search on her cellphone. The woman lived two hours away in Summerville, Alabama.

Jessica jumped to her feet and rushed into the bathroom to shower. She would need to hurry if she thought to make the two-hour drive and be back before Owen got home.

* * * *

Summerville, Alabama had to be the quaintest, quietest place Jessica had ever beheld. It boasted of a small, white courthouse in the center of town, with an equally small post office residing next to it.

An old wooden shack sat just off the main stretch with a sign across the top that read: *Emery's BBQ.* The intersection up ahead housed a flashing yellow caution light as well as a four-way-stop. The only thing modern about the town of Summerville was the gold and white convenience store to the right of the intersection.

A few more buildings, such as an auto parts place and a water company, adorned the surrounding area, but Jessica paid little heed. Her mind had zeroed in on her phone and the computerized voice now spouting out her next turn.

She took a left at the intersection, following the signs until she came upon her next turn. Three minutes later, she pulled into what she hoped to be Sandy Weaver's drive.

Opening the back door to her SUV, Jess retrieved the covered painting she'd placed there before leaving the house, and approached the shadowed, screened in porch.

With no visible doorbell in sight, Jess lifted her free hand and rapped her knuckles against the door.

Footsteps could be heard moving through the house, along with the creaking of the floors. The sounds suddenly stopped. "Who's there?"

Jess cleared her throat. "It's Jessica Nobles, Mrs. Weaver. I really need to speak with you."

A long pause ensued, and then, "You came all this way for nothing, Mrs. Nobles. Like I told you on the phone, I got nothing to say."

Jessica rested her forehead against the cool wood of the door. "Please. I won't take up much of your time. I have nowhere else to turn."

The floor squeaked once more, telling Jess that Sandy had taken a step forward.

Raising her head, Jessica backed up a step and watched as the door opened a couple of inches and Sandy's face appeared through the narrow crack.

She peered over Jessica's head as if searching the drive beyond.

"I came alone," Jess quickly assured her. "No one knows I'm here."

The door swung open. "Come in, but please make it brief."

Jessica hesitantly stepped over the threshold, gripping the painting she held as if it were her lifeline. "I'm really sorry for showing up this way, but I didn't know what else to do."

Sandy gestured toward an old, worn looking sofa. "Have a seat."

Nodding her thanks, Jess moved to the couch and lowered her weight onto its center. She propped the covered painting against her legs and waited for Sandy to sit as well.

Sandy Weaver looked nothing like Jessica had imagined. She'd expected the woman to have long, unkept hair and dress like a gypsy, but instead, she sported a short, blonde pixie, a purple T-shirt and snug fitting jeans.

"Can I offer you a drink?"

At Jessica's polite refusal, Sandy took a seat in a faded brown recliner and lit up a cigarette. "What is it that you need from me?"

"Tell me about what you saw after Terry Dayton's disappearance."

Sandy took a drag from her cigarette, exhaling her smoke toward the ceiling. "How did you find out about me?"

"I spoke with the reporter who covered the Dayton case. He told me what you saw in the upstairs window of the Dayton house."

Taking another puff from the cigarette, Sandy briefly closed her eyes and then pierced Jess with a penetrating stare. "I can't be involved in this. I left that neighborhood for a reason."

"Tell me."

"Eustice Martin."

Jessica's heart jumped into her throat. "I've had a couple of run-ins with him."

"If you were smart, you'd go as far from Sparkleberry Hills as you can get."

"Do you think Eustice killed that Dayton boy?" Jessica leaned forward on the sofa, searching the other woman's gaze.

Sandy jumped to her feet and began to pace. "So, you know the boy's dead too."

Jessica stood as well, removed the covering from the painting and held it up where Sandy could see it.

"Jesus," Sandy breathed, her attention locked on the painting of Terry's small body in that grave. "Where did you get that?"

"I painted it one night after I'd blacked out. I have no recollection of how it came to be. I only know that I woke with the paintbrush in my hand and this image on the canvas in front of me."

Tears filled Sandy's eyes. "I saw the exact same thing. When I told the police what I'd seen, they investigated me like I had something to do with his disappearance."

"I'm sorry," Jessica whispered, setting the painting down next to the sofa. "What do you think it means, and why did I see it too? Nothing like this has ever happened to me before."

Sandy wiped at her tears with trembling fingers and crushed out her cigarette in the ashtray beside her chair. "My best guess would be that you're an open channel. Probably due to the overwhelming grief you're experiencing from the loss of your child."

Jessica stilled. "I never said anything about losing a child."

"You didn't have to. As I said on the phone, I knew why you'd called. I also know that you can't move beyond the death of your son. It eats away at you like a cancer, slowly devouring your mind as well as your will to live."

All the air left Jessica's lungs, deflating her to the point, she had no choice but to return to her seat or fall on her face. "His name was Jacob. He was seven years old when he passed away."

"He was your only child." It wasn't a question.

Jessica weakly nodded. "My husband wanted to have another baby, but I couldn't do it. No one could ever replace Jacob."

Sandy moved around the coffee table and sat down next to Jess on the sofa. She took hold of Jessica's hands and tugged her around to face her.

A faraway look entered Sandy's eyes. "You have severed the bond you once had with your husband. Though he holds tight to it, refusing to let go."

"Yes…"

"There has been no intimacy," Sandy continued, coasting her thumbs along Jess's palms. "You have lost the ability to love, to trust…to feel."

Jess swallowed hard, unable to speak.

Releasing her hold on Jessica's hands, Sandy picked up the painting and held it up in front of her. "Terry Dayton is buried in this grave. Of that, you can be certain."

Chapter Fourteen

Jessica sat in Sandy Weaver's living room, unable to look away from the woman's strained profile.

Sandy had just confirmed what Jess already knew. The boy who'd once lived in that two-story house hadn't merely disappeared, he'd been murdered. "Where is this grave, and who put him there?"

Returning the painting next to the couch, Sandy shrugged. "If I had those answers, the police would have found his remains by now."

"But you're a psychic," Jessica argued, unwilling to believe that Sandy didn't know anything. "How can you see his grave but not know its location?"

Sandy laughed without humor. "It doesn't work that way. I only know what I'm shown. I can't make the images appear at will. If I could, do you think I'd be living like this?" She waved her hand out in a wide arc.

Jessica considered her words. "Okay, so you don't know where he's buried, but you must have some idea of who put him there."

"I have no proof, but I believe Eustice Martin is involved."

Jess had wondered the same thing. "Aside from him being the world's largest asshat, what makes you think Eustice had something to do with it?"

"He threatened me."

"Just because he threatened you doesn't make him a murderer. Although, I would be willing to bet the farm that he is."

Sandy got to her feet and lit up another cigarette. "It was no mere threat to me, it was made toward my boys."

The reporter had mentioned that Sandy had children. "Go on."

"After I'd told the police what I'd seen, I confided in Terry's parents. They, of course, thought I was insane, and Melanie attacked me."

Jess held up a hand. "Melanie, Terry's mother? And attacked you how?"

Sandy began to pace once more. "Yes, the child's mother. She became inconsolable, screaming and crying, and then she threw herself at me. It took her husband and one other man there to pull her off me."

"Oh, my God," Jess breathed, picturing the scene in her mind. "What did you do?"

"The only thing I could do. I got out of there and ran home. Later that night, Eustice showed up at my place wielding a gun. He told me if I opened my mouth about the Dayton boy once more, he'd turn the gun on my boys."

Jessica's mouth dropped open. "Did you go to the police?"

Sandy shook her head, but never slowed her pacing. "I was going to until I dreamed that night that I saw my youngest son buried in the same grave as Terry."

Surging to her feet, Jessica skirted the coffee table and placed herself in Sandy's path. "That's proof enough that Eustice killed Terry. How else would you have seen your son buried in that same grave after Eustice Martin's threat against your boys?"

Sandy stopped her pacing and held Jessica's gaze. "You're right, yet I can't help but feel there's something I'm missing. I don't know what it is, but I believe there's more to it than Eustice killing Terry for the hell of it."

"Maybe Terry saw something he wasn't supposed to?" Jess offered, grasping at straws.

Snuffing out her cigarette, Sandy moved to the door, twisted the knob and threw it open. "I've done all I can do to help you. Please... just go now."

Jessica picked up the painting and trailed to the open door. She stopped on the porch and turned to face Sandy. "If you see anything else, would you please call me?"

"I'm sorry, I really am, but I've said all I'm going to say. If Eustice Martin finds out that I spoke to you, he'll hunt me down and make good on his threat."

"I would never tell him that I saw you. You needn't worry about that."

Sandy didn't look convinced. "He has ways of finding out your every move. That whole damn neighborhood does." She closed the door in Jessica's face.

Jess glanced at her watch on her way to her SUV. She still had five hours before Owen came home from work which left her enough time to pay Ruckle a visit.

She carefully set the painting in the backseat, climbed behind the wheel, and backed out of the drive.

Chapter Fifteen

Jessica sat in the back-corner booth at Happy's Bar and Grill, waiting patiently for Steven Ruckle's arrival. She'd thought about everything that she would tell him on her trip back to Sparkleberry Hills.

The bell rang above the door, drawing Jessica's attention.

Steven Ruckle sent her a nod while weaving his way through the crowd. He sat down across from her.

The waitress appeared, but he casually waved her away before meeting Jessica's gaze. "Has something happened?"

"You could say that. I met with Sandy Weaver this morning."

Surprise registered in Steven's eyes. "I thought she left this area?"

"She did. It was a good two-hour drive from here."

He leaned back in his seat and loosened his tie. "How did that go?"

"Not good. She was terrified that my showing up there would lead Eustice Martin to her door. I tried to assure her that he wouldn't find out."

A muscle ticked along Steven's jaw. "She was right to be terrified. Eustice isn't someone to play with. He spent the first ten years of his adult life in prison for killing a man."

Jessica's eyes widened. "What? That's the first I've heard of it. How did he only get ten years?"

"Crime of passion. He supposedly caught the guy with his fiancée." Steven ran a hand through his light brown hair and softened his gaze. "Look, I'm going to give you some friendly advice here. Leave it alone. The boy's been missing for thirteen years, he's not coming back. He—"

"He's dead," Jessica blurted, cutting him off. "And I'm fairly sure that Eustice Martin murdered him." Jess went on to tell Steven everything she'd learned from her visit with Sandy Weaver, ending with, "He threatened her at gunpoint. He also threatened her children."

Steven blew out a breath and leaned back in his seat. "I knew her packing up and leaving in the middle of the night had something to do with Eustice."

"It had everything to do with him." Jessica reached beneath the table and tugged her painting up onto the seat next to her.

"What is that?" Steven nodded to half hidden painting.

"Proof that Terry is dead."

Steven simply stared back at her with a blank expression.

"I painted this one night shortly after we'd moved into the neighborhood. I have no recollection of doing it. I'd sat down to paint my son and the next thing I knew, my husband was standing in the doorway, calling my name."

Steven's eyebrows lifted. "I didn't know you had a son."

"He died three years ago," Jessica murmured, speaking the words for the first time in three years without tearing up.

"I'm sorry, Mrs. Nobles."

Jessica nodded her thanks, her mind still racing from everything she'd learned at Sandy Weaver's place. "The point I'm trying to make here is that I somehow blacked out and painted the very scene that Sandy Weaver saw all those years back."

Steven jerked his chin toward the painting. "Let's see it."

Gripping the sides of the canvas, Jess hoisted it up to give him a better look.

"That's the Dayton boy," Steven unnecessarily pointed out. "But a painting of a child lying in a grave isn't proof of anything as far as the police are concerned. And if you tell anyone else about it, they'll think you're as nuts as poor Sandy Weaver."

Jessica set the painting next to her on the booth seat. "I am nuts, Mr. Ruckle. I have been ever since my son passed away. I really couldn't give a damn what anyone thinks of me, but my husband doesn't deserve the stigma of my insanity attached to his name. I wasn't planning on turning it in."

Instead of the uncomfortable look she'd expected to get from Steven about her statement, he merely rested his hands on the tabletop and leaned forward. "I'd love to find the Dayton boy as much as you, but without any evidence or even a few concrete leads, we're just spinning our wheels. I searched for Terry Dayton for three years, dug around in everyone's business on that street—both legally and illegally. I uncovered many secrets I'm sure they'd rather not have told, but I never found any evidence on who took Terry."

"I know this painting isn't considered evidence to you, Mr. Ruckle, but it is to me. Especially after finding out that Sandy saw the same thing thirteen years ago."

"Please, call me Steven."

Taken aback for a moment, Jessica paused before continuing. "Sandy doesn't believe that Eustice was alone in what happened to Terry. She seems to think there was someone else involved."

"Did she say why she thought that?"

Jess shook her head. "Not really. She said it was more of a gut feeling, and I'm inclined to trust her gut after everything she told me." Jess quickly repeated her conversation with Sandy. "If she does know more, she's staying tight lipped about it. Not that I blame her."

Steven glanced at his watch. "I'm going to have to run. I have a meeting in ten minutes."

He reached across the table and wrapped his warm fingers around Jessica's wrist when she moved to get up. "I have access to a lot that never got printed in the papers. I also have friends on the force who worked the Dayton case. I'll see if there's anything that got overlooked during the investigation."

Jess sent him a grateful look. "Thank you, Steven. It means a lot."

"No problem." He gave her hand a gentle squeeze. "Stay as low-key as you can until you hear from me. I'll be in touch."

Jessica watched him go with more than a little relief inside. Not only had he believed her theory on what happened to Terry Dayton, but he hadn't batted an eye when she'd confided in him about how the painting came to be. He believed in her, and that felt better than she could have imagined it would.

Chapter Sixteen

"How was your day?" Owen lay in bed, flipping through the channels on the television.

Jessica wanted to tell him everything that had happened since he'd left for work that morning, but she couldn't. He would only become angry and probably insist she get back on her meds. "It was okay."

He turned off the TV and rolled to his side to face her. "Something is different with you."

"What do you mean?"

Owen shrugged. "I'm not sure. Did you cut your hair?"

"No. I applied a little makeup this morning. Maybe that's what you're seeing."

A sleepy smile touched his lips. "That's probably it."

He leaned in and kissed her. "Goodnight, Jess."

"Night, Owen." Jess remained completely still, staring up at the shadows on the ceiling and listening to Owen's soft breathing. It didn't take long before the expected snoring ensued.

She inched back the covers, careful not to shake the bed, and got to her feet. She hated sneaking around behind Owen's back, but he honestly left her no choice.

Back in the office, Jess seated herself in front of her desk and turned on the laptop. She typed in Jasper and Melanie Dayton, steadily glancing at the door while the page loaded.

A black and white photo appeared of the Dayton's holding a press conference. The date below the image told Jessica the conference had been held four days after Terry's disappearance.

The distraught look in Melanie's eyes tore at Jessica's heart. Jess knew all too well the pain Mrs. Dayton had felt in that moment. Nothing could ever come close to the agony of losing a child.

Jessica's gaze touched on Jasper Dayton, taking note of the protective way his arm held tightly to his wife.

Jasper Dayton had been a handsome man thirteen years ago with his dark, semi-long hair and masculine jawline. He appeared to be tall as well, standing a good foot above his dainty wife.

Handsome couple, Jessica thought, clicking back and then onto the next link. A picture of the Dayton house appeared in the article currently loading. It amazed Jessica, how much it had changed over the years. Little Terry Dayton had lived in that house, probably felt safe, happy, and loved.

Jessica wasn't sure how long she sat there scrolling through the different articles once again before her aching back demanded she get up and move around.

She ventured out into the living room, drawn to the front window like a moth to a flame.

With the glare of the streetlight shining in her eyes, Jess cupped her hands around her face and pressed her forehead to the glass. There, looking back at her from the second story window of the abandoned house, stood Terry Dayton.

Jess squeezed her eyes tightly shut, counted to ten and then eased them back open to find the Dayton boy…gone.

Doubt quickly surfaced. What if all of this was a figment of her imagination and she was back in Chicago, rocking in a corner somewhere in an institution?

She trailed over to the door, disengaged the locks, and stepped outside.

Though the night felt warm, a gentle breeze blew through the trees to cool Jessica's bare legs.

Moving off the porch, she inched down the driveway, never taking her gaze from the window of that house.

"Looking for something?"

Jessica sucked in a startled breath and spun to face the owner of that deep voice.

A tall, blond man stood in the street wearing jean-cutoff shorts and a tank top. He held a can of beer in one hand while flipping a knife in the other.

"I—I—no, I was just taking a short walk." She couldn't look away from that knife.

The man glanced toward the Dayton house and then resettled his gaze on her. "Seems to me you were looking for something in that house over there. Now, what could be so interesting that you would be out here at midnight, creeping around to see?"

"I wasn't creeping," she whispered, backing up a step. "I told you, I was — "

"Out getting some air. So you say."

Jess eased back another step. "Well, as you said, it's rather late. I'll bid you a goodnight, then."

He didn't respond. He simply stood there, flipping that knife in his left hand and staring at her through bloodshot eyes.

Once Jessica backed far enough away, she spun on her heel and fled to the safety of her house.

Throwing the deadbolt home, she scurried to the window to find the blond man staggering down the street, still flipping that knife.

She watched for several minutes more, taking note of which house he stumbled up to, before turning away from the window and heading to bed.

Chapter Seventeen

Owen sat in his office at the First Bank and Trust of Sparkleberry Hills sucking down his third cup of coffee.

He pushed back his chair and stood, stretching his muscles and fighting a yawn. He hadn't slept worth a damn last night. Every time he'd rolled toward Jessica in his sleep, he would find her gone. Figuring she was in the office painting, he'd left her alone and attempted sleep once more.

A knock sounded on his door.

"Come in," Owen called, smoothing his tie before returning to his seat.

Brenda, his secretary, stuck her head inside. "You have a visitor."

Owen lifted an eyebrow. "A visitor?"

The secretary nodded. "A Mrs. Hawthorn. Says she's your neighbor."

"Send her in." Owen couldn't imagine what his casserole making neighbor could possibly want with him.

Marge Hawthorn bustled into the room wearing a bright yellow pantsuit. "I do apologize for barging in on you like this, but I felt it important enough to speak with you about in person."

"No need for apologies," Owen assured her while waving a hand toward the chair in front of his desk. "Please, have a seat."

Closing the door behind her, Marge strode across the room and lowered her ample weight into the chair. "I appreciate you seeing me."

"What can I do for you, Mrs. Hawthorn?"

She made a big show of smoothing her pants around her knees. "It's about your wife."

Owen's stomach tightened with dread. "Is she alright? Has something happened?"

"Oh no, Mr. Nobles, I'm sure she's fine. It's just that…"

"Go on," Owen urged, attempting to keep the impatience from his voice.

Marge blew out a breath and clasped her hands in her lap. "She's been acting rather strange, lately."

"Strange, as in?"

"Well, for starters, I see her outside at all times of the night. Usually staring at the abandoned house next door to you. Then last night around midnight, I noticed her standing in the street talking to Dale Schroder. Looked to me like they were arguing about something."

Owen couldn't believe what he was hearing. Surely to God, Jessica wasn't sneaking out of the house at night! Furthermore, what was their busybody neighbor doing up at that time of night watching his wife's every move?

He cleared his throat, wondering what to say to Marge without coming across as an asshole. "I appreciate you letting me know, Mrs. Hawthorn. Jessica doesn't sleep very well since our son's passing."

Marge paled. "Oh dear. I am so sorry to hear that. I had no idea. Please accept my deepest sympathies."

"Thank you," Owen murmured, hating the pity he saw in Mrs. Hawthorn's eyes. "We lost Jacob a little over three years ago."

Marge blinked back tears. "I'm really sorry to have come here like this. Had I known..." She touched her throat and tried again. "My apologies."

Gaining her feet, Marge's mouth opened and closed without sound. She reached into her pants pocket and withdrew a handkerchief. "Have a nice day, Mr. Nobles."

"You too, Mrs. Hawthorn."

"Marge. Call me Marge." She turned and left without another word.

It took Owen several minutes to calm down enough to pick up the phone. He quickly dialed Jessica's cell only to reach her voicemail.

Gathering up the papers in front of him, Owen tucked them away in the top drawer of his desk and stood. He glanced at the clock on the wall. It was a little before ten AM. After being up half the night, Jess was probably sleeping.

He'd find out soon enough.

* * * *

Owen pulled into his driveway, immediately noticing the garage door had been left open and Jessica's SUV was nowhere in sight.

Leaving his own car running, he jumped out, unlocked the door to the house, and hurried inside.

The scent of perfume permeated the air, surprising him. Jess hadn't worn perfume in as long as he could remember.

He approached the closet, noticing a pair of heels missing from her shoe rack. Jealousy ensued.

Jessica hadn't wanted anything to do with him in years, yet she'd apparently dressed up, smelled like a million bucks, and wasn't answering her phone.

Owen dug out his cell from the pocket of his pants and tried her again. *Voicemail.*

He pressed the end key and typed out a text. *Tried calling a couple of times. Where are you?*

No reply.

Had she met someone in town and was now in his arms?

Owen shook his head at the direction of his thoughts. Jessica would never cheat on him. *Would she?*

Chapter Eighteen

Jessica stopped her SUV along the curbside of Jasper and Melanie Dayton's house. At least she hoped it belonged to them. She'd called Ruckle and talked him into giving her their address.

She sat outside for several minutes, trying to work up the nerve to get out, when the front door to the house opened and a petite blonde exited the home.

Quickly climbing from the SUV, Jessica strode across the yard, her high heels sinking into the freshly mowed grass of the manicured lawn. "Mrs. Dayton?"

The blonde woman stopped, surprise registering on her face. "I'm sorry. Do I know you?"

"No," Jessica admitted, reaching the woman's side. "My name's Jessica Nobles. Do you have a minute?"

Melanie gave a curt nod. "I was just about to head into town. What can I do for you?"

"I wanted to speak with you about your son, Terry."

A shadow passed through Melanie's eyes. "Are you a reporter?"

"I'm not. I moved into the house next door to your old place. I'd like to ask you some questions, if you don't mind?"

Melanie hesitated a moment and then waved a hand toward the house. "Would you care to come inside?"

"Thank you. That would be great." Jessica followed the pretty blonde through the front door of a pale yellow, stucco home. The first thing she noticed were the lack of pictures in the front room. Not one photograph of Terry adorned the walls or any of the tables that made up the large space.

Melanie gestured to the sofa. "Please, have a seat. What is it that you would like to know?"

Jessica waited for Melanie to sit in a straight-back chair before lowering herself onto the sofa, facing her. "I'm really not sure where to begin. Let me start off by saying how sorry I am for your loss."

"I appreciate your kind words, Mrs. Nobles, but Terry isn't dead. He's missing. I would know if he were dead." She rubbed her palms over her knees. "I wouldn't expect you to understand."

Holding Melanie's gaze, Jess responded softly, "I do understand. I lost my only child a little over three years ago. He was seven years old when he passed."

Melanie paled. "I'm so sorry. I had no idea. I—"

"You're fine, Mrs. Dayton. There was no way you could have known."

An awkward silence fell. Jessica nervously cleared her throat. "Tell me about Terry."

A faraway look entered Melanie's eyes. "He's twenty years old now, did you know that? It's hard to wrap my mind around. I often try to imagine what he looks like today, but I can't. In my mind's eye, he's still the seven-year-old little boy who went missing so long ago."

"The newspaper articles stated that he was taken in the middle of the night. It also said there were suspicions surrounding his disappearance."

Melanie's eyes sharpened, losing the lost look they'd exhibited only seconds before. "Yes. There was this woman who lived across the street—this psychic they were looking into. Also, Eustice Martin. Have you met him yet?"

"Unfortunately, I have."

"Well, then you've seen what type of person he is."

Jessica nodded. "I know that he's been in prison for murder and that he abuses his wife."

"Why are you interested in Terry?" Melanie suddenly asked, catching Jessica off guard.

Wondering how much to reveal of what she'd seen, Jessica hedged, "Since finding out about your son and what happened in that house next door to me, I haven't been able to think of much else. I've read everything the internet has to offer on the investigation, and I couldn't help but wonder if Eustice had something to do with his disappearance."

"I understand your curiosity, Mrs. Nobles, but why would you want to get involved?"

Jessica looked down at her fingernails. Her heart began to pound, and her palms grew sweaty. She decided to be honest with Mrs. Dayton. If the woman threw her out on her ear, then so be it. "I saw him."

"Saw who?"

Jessica lifted her head. "Your son."

"You—" Melanie's mouth opened and closed several times. "You saw Terry?"

"More than once..."

All the color drained from Melanie's face. "Where? When? I don't understand!"

Jessica recognized the signs of a panic attack, and Mrs. Dayton was definitely on the verge of one.

Surging to her feet, Jessica skirted the coffee table that sat between them and touched Melanie on the shoulder. "This is going to sound crazy, but I need you to please hear me out."

Melanie raised a tear-filled gaze but remained silent.

"I…" Clearing her throat, Jess tried again. "I saw him in the upstairs window of the house next door to me. Your old house."

When Melanie didn't respond, Jess continued. "He-he had dark hair, and he was wearing a striped T-shirt. I saw him the first night I moved into the house next door."

Melanie pushed to her feet, forcing Jess to take a step back. "You came here today to tell me that you saw the ghost of my son Terry?"

"I know it sounds crazy, Mrs. Dayton, and I wish to God I had a different reason for being here, but I don't. I know what I saw, and I've seen him more than once."

"Please leave."

Jessica's heart ached for this woman who'd lost her child. She ached for the sadness Melanie tried to hide, the deep grief that lay just beneath the surface. "I didn't come here to upset you. I came here hoping that I could help."

Melanie marched to the door and held it open. "You can help by not contacting me again."

"Sandy Weaver saw the same things I did. Things that didn't make the papers, things I had no way of knowing about."

Something flickered in Melanie's gaze. "How do you know what Sandy saw?"

"Because I saw her."

"Saw her where? She left the area thirteen years ago. Just up and disappeared in the middle of the night."

Jessica stopped at the open door but remained inside. "She lives in Summerville, Alabama. I paid her a visit to reveal to her what I'd seen. I had no idea that she'd seen the same things."

"I don't know what sort of game you're playing, Mrs. Nobles, but I want no part of it. Now, good day."

"Melanie, please…"

"Go."

With an apologetic nod, Jessica stepped out onto the porch, the click of the door closing, echoing behind her.

Unsure of what to do next, Jess jogged to her SUV, grabbed a pen and paper from her purse, and wrote down her cellphone number. She strode back across the yard and slipped the paper beneath the door.

Chapter Nineteen

Owen sat on the couch facing the door when the sound of a car pulling into the drive reached his ears. Jessica was home.

He remained seated, waiting on her to enter the house. He'd been calling her cell and texting her for hours to no avail.

The door opened and she stepped inside. "What are you doing home?"

"Waiting on you. Where have you been?"

She closed the door and turned to face him. "In town. Why?"

"I've been calling and texting you for hours. What good is having a cellphone if you never use it?"

Stepping out of her heels, she bent, picked them up, and flipped her hair over her shoulder. "What's with the third degree?"

Anger quickly replaced his concern. "Why are you evading my questions?"

"I left my cell in the car, Owen. Are we really going to argue over that fact?"

Owen surged to his feet. "You've been acting strange for weeks...up all hours of the night, arguing with neighbors in the street."

Her eyes narrowed. "Arguing with the neighbors? If you're referring to Eustice Martin, I—"

"I'm talking about Dale Schroder. Why the hell were you standing in the street having words with him after midnight? Furthermore, why didn't you tell me about it?"

She stared at him for long moments before blowing out a defeated breath. "I wasn't standing in the street arguing. I'd stepped outside to get some air when he approached me at the end of the drive. He'd been drinking and was simply running his mouth. It had nothing to do with you. I handled it just fine."

"I'm a local bank manager, Jessica. Everything you do reflects back on me."

"Are you kidding me?" she snapped, taking a step closer. "You're worried I'll make you look bad to the local gossips? Jesus, Owen. It was a simple misunderstanding with a drunk."

"It's more than that and you know it, Jess. You've been traipsing around outside in the middle of the night since we moved here."

Her mouth dropped open. "What are you doing, creeping around to watch my every move?"

"I don't have to. People talk, Jess. Especially in small towns like this."

"Well, maybe you should have thought about that before you moved us here!" She spun on her heel and stormed off down the hall.

Owen followed. "Where did you go this morning?"

"I told you," she bit out, entering their bedroom. "Into town."

"For what? What did you do in town? You didn't shop, I checked the bank account."

She tossed her shoes into the closet and squared off with him. "You're spying on me, now? Checking the accounts? How about the mileage on my car, have you checked that too?"

"Do I need to?" he shouted, growing angrier by the second. "What are you hiding from me? And don't lie to me, Jess. Your right eye always twitches when you lie, exactly as it's doing now."

Jessica pinched the bridge of her nose and lowered her head. "Fine. I went to see Melanie Dayton."

"Who the hell is Melanie Dayton?"

She jerked her thumb toward the bedroom window. "The woman who used to own that house next door."

Though still angry, Owen took a calming breath and moved to sit on the edge of the bed. "What made you go see the woman who used to live next door?"

Jess lifted her head to reveal moisture swimming in her eyes. "You wouldn't understand, Owen."

"Try me." It pained his heart to see Jessica's tears.

She moved to sit next to him on the bed. He noticed her hands trembled. "Remember the boy I saw in the house next door the night I was accosted by Eustice Martin?"

At Owen's nod, she continued. "That wasn't a random neighborhood child I saw. It was Terry Dayton."

Owen thought about that for a moment. "It couldn't have been the Dayton boy, Jess. He would be an adult by now."

"I know," she sniffled, picking at her thumb nail. "But it was him. I looked up his disappearance on the internet. There's no doubt in my mind that the child was Terry Dayton. He even wore the same striped T-shirt Terry had on when he went missing."

Owen's heart cracked. The longer he sat there, listening to her story, the more he realized he was losing her. She sounded paranoid, delusional…insane. "Ah, Jess…"

"You think I'm crazy." She stood and moved to the window facing the Dayton house.

"I don't think you're crazy, Jess. I believe that you think you saw something in that house. But the missing Dayton boy couldn't be it. He's been gone for thirteen years."

Owen left the bed to stand behind his wife. He wrapped his arms around her and rested his chin on the top of her head. "I think we should see a doctor."

Jessica broke free of his hold and stepped out of his reach. "That is exactly why I can't tell you anything, Owen. You think drugs are the answer to everything. The bottom line here is that you don't trust me. Well, guess what? I don't trust you either."

She stormed from the room, leaving Owen standing by that window.

"What are you doing?" Owen questioned softly as she marched back in and grabbed her shoes from the closet.

She stopped at the bedroom door, her back remaining to him. "I'm going for a drive."

Chapter Twenty

Tears dripped down Jessica's face as she backed out of the driveway and headed west. In the weeks that she'd been in Sparkleberry Hills, she'd experienced nothing but insanity. At least in Chicago, she'd had Dr. Knox to turn to when things got bad.

She wiped at her tear-soaked cheeks with the back of her hand and jerked up her cellphone.

Scrolling through the alphabet, Jess found the doctor's name and pressed the call key.

"Doctor Knox's office," his secretary answered on the second ring.

Jessica pressed the cell firmly against her ear to keep her hand from trembling. She opened her mouth to speak, but the words wouldn't come. What the hell was she going to tell the doctor, anyway? *Hey, I'm seeing the ghost of a missing neighborhood boy. And he just happens to be the same age as Jacob.*

"Hello? Dr. Knox's office," the secretary repeated.

Jessica took a fortifying breath. "This is Jessica Nobles. Is Doctor Knox in?"

"He's just finishing up with a patient. Would you like to leave a message?"

"I," Jessica began, only to falter.

The secretary spoke to someone in a low tone before announcing. "The doctor is free now, Mrs. Nobles. Hold please."

Jessica's stomach lurched. She suddenly wished she hadn't dialed the psychologist's office.

"Mrs. Nobles?" The doctor's deep, soothing voice came over the line. "What can I do for you?"

Jess hesitated before losing her nerve altogether. "I'm sorry for bothering you."

She quickly pressed the end key and tossed the cell onto the passenger's seat.

It buzzed almost instantly, the vibrating sound muffled by the cloth of the seat.

Jess let it ring out, and then plucked it up and called Ruckle. "I need to see you."

"Come by my office. I'm just finishing up some things." He rattled off the address.

"Be there in ten."

For some reason the thought of seeing Steven Ruckle calmed her nerves a little. She supposed it had to do with the fact that he didn't judge her. He simply let her talk things out, offered help where he could, and didn't push.

Jess returned her cell to the passenger seat and gripped the wheel with both hands. She had a ten-minute drive ahead of her, and she planned to use that time to regain some of her composure.

* * * *

"Hey," Steven greeted, his fingers flying over a keyboard. "Have a seat. I'll be right with you."

Jessica sat in one of the two chairs in front of his desk. She let her gaze sweep his spacious office, taking in the numerous plaques and certificates hanging on the walls.

The sounds of typing suddenly stopped. "All done. What's up, Mrs. Nobles?"

"I really wish you would call me Jessica."

He grinned, making his normally appealing face, downright handsome. "Yes, ma'am."

Jess relaxed, somewhat and returned his smile. "I paid a visit to Melanie Dayton, today."

Steven's smile faltered. "How did that go?"

"Not good. I told her about my sightings. Needless to say, she wasn't happy about it."

"I imagine not. From what I heard, she flipped out on Sandy Weaver for her psychic claims of seeing Terry."

Jessica shifted in her seat. "They weren't merely claims. Sandy really did see what she said she did. She even saw the same thing that I saw. But I'm no psychic."

"Then what do you call seeing ghosts in windows and painting shallow graves?"

"Crazy?"

Steven shrugged. "Could be, but I doubt it. I believe there are people walking this earth with the gift of seeing things that are beyond our comprehension. In fact, we are probably all capable of it on some deeper level. Only most of us wouldn't begin to know how to reach into that part of ourselves."

"I'd give anything to be like everyone else," Jessica whispered. "I feel like I'm losing my mind. I'm keeping secrets from my husband, slinking around and digging up everything I can on the Dayton investigation. I've become obsessed with it."

Steven's gaze softened. "Although, I've never seen anything even remotely close to a ghost, I do understand obsession. I quickly became obsessed with the Dayton case a week after I began following it. It took me three years and changing jobs to finally learn to move on. And honestly, I can't say that I ever truly did." He abruptly stood. "Come on, let's get out of here."

Jess pushed to her feet as well. "Where are we going?"

"My place."

Chapter Twenty-One

Jessica drove behind Steven's car for several minutes before he took a left off the main road and pulled up onto a circle drive in front of a two-story brick home.

Following suit, Jess parked next to him and got out. "Wow. You live here?"

"No. Here in Sparkleberry Hills, we simply drive around until we find a suitable place to sleep in and take that one."

A laugh bubbled up in Jess, sounding foreign and rusty. She hadn't laughed in years. "Funny."

"It was my parents' place," Steven corrected, waving her up the stone walkway that led to a large overhang.

Jessica trailed up to the front door and stood back while Steven unlocked it.

He pushed it wide. "After you."

She stepped over the threshold. "Where are your parents now?"

"My father died when I was still in my teens, and then mother passed away a few years ago." He closed and locked the door. "Would you like a drink?"

Jess nodded. "That would be great."

"Anything in particular?"

"Whatever you're having is fine."

Steven strode through the foyer toward the kitchen, removing his jacket as he went. He tossed it onto the back of a chair and took down two wine glasses, which he promptly filled with a chardonnay from his fridge.

He handed one to Jessica. "Have a seat."

She sat on a stool at the bar in his kitchen while he stood on the other side sipping his wine.

"Drink that," Steven insisted, nodding toward her glass, "and I'll pour you another."

"I have to drive home."

Steven picked up the bottle of Chardonnay. "You also need to loosen up a bit. You look stressed."

Jessica downed her wine and then held out her glass for a refill which Steven promptly took care of.

Turning back toward the refrigerator, Steven pulled some covered dishes from the bottom shelf and placed them on the bar. He then grabbed two forks and slid one over in front of Jess. "Help me eat this."

Jess laughed for the second time that night. "What is it?"

"Some stuff my neighbors brought over yesterday. I think they feel sorry for me because of my bachelor status."

He peeled back the foil to reveal some barbeque pulled pork, potato salad, and chocolate cake.

Jessica stomach instantly growled. She stabbed some potato salad with her fork and popped it into her mouth. "Mmmmm," she moaned as it slid down her throat. "This is delicious."

She took another bite. "No plates?"

Steven shook his head. "It's easier this way. Besides, it's less mess to clean up afterwards."

Another chuckle escaped her. She could feel the wine warming her insides even as the food filled the emptiness in her stomach. "Thank you for this. I hadn't realized how much I needed some nonjudgmental interaction until now."

"Your husband isn't nonjudgmental?" Steven took a long healthy drink of his wine.

Jess shook her head. "Owen worries about me. A little too much, I think. He means well, but..."

"But what?" Steven prompted, setting his glass aside and digging into the food.

"We have grown apart since Jacob's death. We've somehow become strangers who live under the same roof. I feel like he's always watching me, waiting for me to mess up."

Steven paused with a forkful of food near his mouth. "You ever talk with him about how you feel? Sometimes we men need to be told when we're screwing up. We lack common sense when it comes to relationships."

Jessica loved how easy it was to talk to Steven. His devil-may-care attitude was adorable, not to mention fun. And fun was something she hadn't had in years. "I try to talk with him about it, but it usually ends with us arguing or him suggesting I go see a psychiatrist."

"Ouch. I hate shrinks. They're always watching you over the rim of their glasses like you have a gnat circling your face. And let's not forget the dozens of questions about your mother as if she's the root of all evil."

A deep, belly laugh burst from Jessica with the image Steven created. "That's a psychologist. The psychiatrists are strictly there to pump you full of pills."

She'd said too much. She realized it when Steven's gaze sharpened and he took another drink of his wine.

Setting the glass aside, he asked, "Are you speaking from experience?"

Jessica swallowed the bite of cake she'd just popped into her mouth. The wine she'd recently sucked down seemed to be loosening her tongue. "I was on antianxiety meds for three years. Antidepressants as well as something to help me sleep at night."

Steven leaned forward, resting his elbows on top of the bar. "Because of your son's death?"

"Yeah. I found it too hard to cope without Jacob. I still do at times, but it seems to be getting a little easier. I mean, the pain never goes away, it just becomes more manageable. Which is why Owen is so overprotective. He watched me wither away to nothing, merely existing with suicidal thoughts as a constant companion."

"I'm sorry, Jess."

"Thanks."

Steven twirled his fork around in the barbeque. "So, what's our next move?"

"Our next move?"

"In finding Terry Dayton's killer."

Surprised by Steven's words, Jessica could only stare at him.

"What? You didn't think I would let you search for him by yourself, did you?"

Her fork slid from numb fingers. Jessica jumped from her stool, rounded the bar and wrapped Steven in a hug. "Thank you for not assuming that I'm crazy."

He hugged her back. "I never said you weren't crazy, I only said that I would help you."

She laughed again.

Chapter Twenty-Two

It was well after ten PM when Jessica pulled into the drive to find Owen's car gone.

She switched off the engine, grabbed her keys, and got out in the dark. Owen hadn't turned on the outside light when he'd left.

With only the moonlight to guide her, Jess carefully maneuvered up the walkway to the porch, and slipped her key into the lock. The door pushed inward without her turning the knob. It struck her as odd that Owen would have left without shutting the door completely.

"Owen?" She flipped on the light and staggered back in horror. The sight that greeted her would forever be burned into her brain. Behind the sofa, scrawled in bold, red letters across the wall, were the words: GET OUT.

Jessica stumbled back onto the porch and scrambled to her SUV. She dug out her phone with trembling fingers and dialed 911.

"911 what's your emergency?"

"Send help. Someone's in my home!"

"What is your name and address, ma'am?"

Jessica couldn't think, so great was her fear. It took her a minute to remember her address. "Jessica Nobles. I live at 221 Meadowbrook Circle. Please hurry!"

"Stay on the line with me, ma'am. The police are on the way, okay?"

"Okay," Jessica breathed, her gaze darting around the darkness of her yard.

The dispatcher spoke again, her voice startling Jess. *"Is the subject still in the house?"*

"I don't know. I ran out as soon as I saw the words on the wall."

"Jessica? I need you to get some place safe. Do you have a neighbor's house you can go to until the officers arrive?"

Not knowing which one of her neighbors was responsible for the break in, Jess decided to stay put. "No. But I'm locked in my car."

"Back out of the drive, Jessica. Move your car into the street under the lights."

Jessica cranked her SUV, jerked the gearshift into reverse, and backed into the street. "Okay, I'm in the street now."

"Alright, Jessica, make sure your car doors are locked and do not leave that vehicle for any reason before the officers get there. I'm going to stay on the line with you, alright?"

"Okay," Jess whispered.

The sounds of typing and low speaking voices could be heard coming through the phone.

"Jessica?"

"Yes?"

"*You mentioned some words on a wall. Can you tell me what they were?*"

Jessica swallowed hard. "It said, GET OUT. And I think it was written in blood."

"*You're doing good, Jessica. The officers are almost there.*"

The sound of sirens could be heard turning the corner off the main road. "They're close. I can hear them now."

"*Do you see them?*"

Jess glanced in the rearview mirror in time to see blue and red flashing lights turning on to her street. "Yes, they're here."

"*I'm going to disconnect with you now.*"

Once the call ended, Jessica gripped her phone in her hand and jumped from the vehicle. She waited for the two patrol cars to stop next to her before approaching the closest one.

The officer spoke something into the mic attached to his shoulder and got out. "Mrs. Nobles?"

"Yes."

"Tell me what's going on."

Jessica told him step-by-step everything that had happened from the time she'd pulled into the drive, ending with, "...and that's when I saw the writing on the wall."

"Did you see anyone inside the home?" He slipped his gun free of its holster while the other office joined him.

Jessica shook her head. "No, I immediately ran."

"Get back inside your vehicle while we check it out."

Rushing around the side of her SUV, Jessica climbed back in and dialed Owen. She got his voicemail. "Owen, it's me. Something has happened at the house. I need you to come home as soon as you get this message."

A knock sounded on her window, nearly startling a scream from Jessica. She pressed the automatic button and lowered the glass to face Mrs. Hawthorn.

"What are the police doing here?" Marge breathed, her eyes huge in her face.

"We've had a break in."

Marge slapped a hand over her mouth, her gaze darting toward Jessica's house. She pulled her hand away. "Were you hurt?"

"I'm fine, it just scared the shit out of me."

"Was anything taken?"

Jess shook her head. "I don't know. I came home to find some words written on the wall. I haven't been back inside to check for a possible theft."

The officers picked that moment to step back outside. One of them spoke into his mic while the other approached Jessica's SUV. "We need to take some pictures and dust for fingerprints before you can go inside. Do you have somewhere you can wait? It's going to be a while."

"She can wait at my place," Marge offered, opening the door to the SUV. "I just live right there in the white house trimmed in black."

The officer nodded his understanding and then met Jessica's gaze. "Do you live here alone, ma'am?"

"No. My husband lives here with me."

"Where is he tonight?"

Jessica didn't know. "I'm not sure. I left him a message."

"Alright. I'll come get you when we're done here so that you can do a walk through and make sure nothing's missing."

Jess watched him walk away, her stomach in knots. She glanced over at Mrs. Hawthorn. "I'm ready when you are."

Chapter Twenty-Three

Owen listened to Jessica's message again as he turned onto Meadowbrook Circle. It took him a moment to make out her words and another to see the flashing lights coming from his front yard.

"Shit," he whispered, his heart in his throat. Something had happened to Jess.

He stepped on the gas, speeding the rest of the way to the cul-de-sac. Throwing open his car door, he jumped out and sprinted up the drive. "Jess!"

A police officer quickly stepped in front of him, blocking his entrance into the house. "Whoa. Stand back, sir."

"Where's my wife?" Owen attempted to see around the officer.

"You live here?"

Owen met the officer's gaze. "Yes, this is my home. Where is my wife?"

"She's across the street at the neighbor's house. We suggested she wait there until we finish processing the scene."

Continuing to peer around the officer, Owen's gaze landed on the words written on the wall. "What the hell?"

"Go wait with your wife, sir. We'll be finished here shortly and then you can return home. She's in the white house trimmed in black."

Spinning around, Owen jogged back down the drive, across the street and into Mrs. Hawthorn's yard. He rang the bell.

Marge Hawthorn opened the door, her face full of concern. "She's in the kitchen. Come on in. I'll put on some coffee."

Owen thanked her and hurried inside.

A heavy-set man with graying hair sat at the kitchen table speaking to Jessica in a soothing tone. He stood when Owen entered the room. "I'll just give y'all some time alone."

"Thank you." Owen immediately rushed to Jessica's side, pulled her from her chair, and wrapped her tightly in his arms. "I'm so sorry I wasn't here for you. God, Jess, are you alright?"

"I'm fine. Did you see what was written on the wall?"

Kissing the top of her head, Owen pulled back enough to look into her beautiful eyes. "I saw. Who the hell would do such a thing?"

"I'll tell you who," Marge piped in, stepping into the kitchen. She moved to the counter and picked up the coffee pot. "That Eustice Martin is who."

Fury and helplessness warred inside Owen. He ambled to the opposite side of the counter to face Marge. "Did you see something?"

"No, but I didn't need to. That Eustice is a snake in the grass. The whole neighborhood knows it."

Owen glanced at his wife's pale face before returning his attention to Marge. "But what would Eustice have to gain from breaking into our home?"

Marge shrugged. "Have you stepped on his toes in some way?"

"We called the police on him for knocking his wife around."

"Well, there you have it," Marge stated in a matter-of-fact way.

Owen inhaled the smell of the coffee that began brewing beneath his nose. "What about the people that previously owned our home? Did they ever have trouble with the Martins?"

"The Lovejoys? Not that I recall. Of course, they worked a lot, and so they weren't home during the day much."

Owen watched as Jessica eased over to the window and parted the blinds enough to see out. It tore at his heart to see her so fragile and afraid.

Once the coffee finished brewing, Marge poured them all a cup and then pushed Jessica's toward the edge of the counter before handing one to Owen.

"Thank you." Owen picked up Jessica's coffee and moved to sit at the table.

Jessica joined him, wrapping her hands around the warmth of her cup and meeting Owen's gaze. "This changes everything."

Owen reached out and covered her hand with his. "I know. I'm so sorry, Jess."

She continued as if he hadn't spoken. "I no longer feel safe, Owen. He was in our home, touching our things..."

"We don't know that it was him, Jess. It could have been some neighborhood kids or teenagers who got high and thought it would be funny."

A spark of hope flashed in Jessica's eyes. "Do you think so?"

He didn't, but she didn't need to know that. "If I were a betting man, my money would be on pranking teenagers."

Nearly an hour passed before one of the officers knocked on the Hawthorn's door to inform Owen and Jess that it was safe to return home.

They thanked Mrs. Hawthorn for her hospitality. Owen followed the officer across the street while Jessica moved her SUV into the drive.

Owen's stomach clenched as he stepped over the threshold into his home and took in the words painted on his wall.

Jessica rushed inside, hurrying down the hall, obviously checking the rest of the house for thievery.

"Is that what I think it is?" Owen questioned one of the officers after nodding toward the graffiti.

"It definitely looks like blood. We took some samples to give to the lab. Hopefully, it's not human."

After another ten minutes of speaking with the officers, answering dozens of questions and assuring them he'd call if he found anything missing, Owen walked them to the door. "What happens now?"

"We'll run any fingerprints we found along with the blood samples, and someone will be in touch."

Owen gripped the back of his neck, attempting to relieve some of the tension forming there.

He thanked the officers for their help, closed the door behind them, and turned to stare at the bloody words written on the wall.

A thought entered his mind. Where had Jessica been for the past several hours? Did she know more about what had happened than she was letting on? Worse still, did she have something to do with it?

Guilt flooded Owen the longer he stood there thinking the worst. *Of course Jess had nothing to do with it. Why would she stage something so horrific in her own home? Unless she no longer wishes to stay...*

Owen went in search of his wife.

Chapter Twenty-Four

Jessica looked up as Owen entered their bedroom. "Are the officers gone?"

Owen nodded. "I'll clean up the wall before I go to bed. It may leave a stain, but nothing a touch up of paint won't take care of."

Jess noticed a strange look in his eyes as if he had something to say yet held back. "What is it?"

He moved up next to the dresser, propped his hip against the side, and picked up a bottle of her perfume.

Bringing the fragrance to his nose, he inhaled deeply and met her gaze. "Where did you go tonight?"

She wasn't about to mention Steven. Not that she'd done anything wrong, but Owen probably wouldn't believe that. "I walked around the mall. Why?"

"Are you sure about that?" He carefully returned the perfume to its previous spot.

Jessica's stomach tightened. She hated like hell lying to Owen. "Yes, I'm sure. Where were you?"

"At a bar," he answered without hesitation. "Having a drink."

"Why do you ask, Owen? You've been suspicious of my every move since we arrived in this godforsaken place."

He crossed his arms over his chest, holding her gaze without blinking. "Ah, yes, this *godforsaken* place. Do you really hate it so much?"

"No, I don't hate it."

"It's no secret that you're not happy here, Jess. In fact, you made it quite clear that you didn't want to move to Florida to begin with."

"Owen, I—"

"Did you set this whole thing up?"

Momentarily speechless, Jessica blinked. "Are you asking me what I think you are?"

"Did you stage this entire scene tonight?" he continued, the accusation hanging in the air.

Jessica's last thread of control snapped. "You son of a bitch! Do you really think I'm capable of something so despicable? After all these years of marriage, you honestly don't know me at all."

She strode toward the door, only to come up short as he caught her by the arm and spun her to face him. "Answer the question, Jess. Did you leave those words on the wall in there?"

"Screw you," she seethed, twisting her arm free of his hold. "Screw you and this town!"

Storming from the room, Jess snatched up her purse along with her keys and marched to her SUV with Owen tight on her heels.

"Go ahead and run, Jess. That's what you're best at, isn't it?"

She jerked her car door open and turned to face him. "Apparently so, Owen. Maybe you should ask yourself why that is? If someone is running, they have to be running from something or someone, don't they?"

Climbing into the SUV, Jessica tossed her purse onto the passenger's seat and reached to close the door. "I'll come by tomorrow and pick up some of my things."

Owen prevented her from closing the door. Though he looked angry, she could see the anxiety lurking just beneath the surface as if he feared he'd gone too far. "Where are you going to go?"

"Anywhere but here."

"So, that's it. You're leaving me? No talking it out?"

"Do you really care? Why would you want someone here capable of the things you accused me of?"

"Jess…"

"Move," she bit out, putting the SUV in reverse.

Left with no choice but to get out of the way or get ran over, Owen backed away.

It wasn't until Jessica reached the intersection, that she allowed the tears to freely flow. Owen believed her responsible for leaving that message on the wall. Whatever bond that had remained after Jacob's death, had finally severed under the pressure.

* * * *

Jess had been up most of the night, pacing the floor of the small motel she'd rented. She had waited until time for Owen to leave for work before driving to the house to grab a few of her things. She couldn't stay at the motel indefinitely, but it would be a roof over her head until she could decide what to do next.

Turning onto Meadowbrook Circle, Jess noticed a couple of patrol cars parked at the edge of her yard.

She pulled into the drive, taking in the Alabama plates on one of the vehicles.

Snagging her purse, she hoisted it onto her shoulder and exited her SUV. Two officers followed suit, one of them female.

"Jessica Nobles?" the female inquired as she approached.

At Jessica's nod, the woman extended her hand. "I'm Detective Vickerson, ma'am." She gestured to her companion. "And this is Officer Dunlap with the Sparkleberry Hills Police Department."

Jessica accepted her outstretched palm, curious as to what an Alabama law enforcement official would be doing at her house. "Is this about the break in?"

Detective Vickerson shook her head. "Would you mind coming with us to the station? We need to ask you a few questions."

What could they possibly need to ask her about at the station that they couldn't ask her now? "What sort of questions?"

"We'll fill you in on everything once we reach the station. Please, come with me."

Taking hold of Jessica's elbow, Vickerson guided her toward the squad car with the Alabama plates and opened the back door. "Watch your head."

Chapter Twenty-Five

The ride to the station had been excruciating for Jessica. No matter how many times she'd inquired about her reason for being in the back of that patrol car, the detective had refused to tell her.

Now, there she sat in a small interrogation room at the local police station, still in the proverbial dark.

The door opened, and the detective stepped inside. She pulled out a chair, taking a seat across the table from Jess.

"Why have I been brought here?" Jess demanded, nervous and more than a little confused. "Am I being arrested for something?"

Vickerson held a yellow folder in her hands, which she promptly placed on the table in front of her. "You're not under arrest, Mrs.

Nobles. We just need to ask you some questions."

"About what?" Wrapping her arms around her waist, Jessica watched the detective open the folder and retrieve a piece of paper.

"What is your relationship with Sandy Weaver?"

The question caught Jessica off guard. Why would they be asking her about Sandy? "I don't have a relationship with Mrs. Weaver. I barely know her."

"You barely know her," Vickerson repeated. "Then how do you explain your number in her cell phone? It looks as if you were the last person she spoke with by phone."

What were the cops doing with Sandy Weaver's phone? Jess wondered, surprised by the question. "I called Mrs. Weaver a few days ago. What is going on?"

"What did you talk about?" the detective continued, ignoring Jessica's question.

Jess couldn't possibly tell them the reason for her phone call to Sandy. They would think her a lunatic. So, she hedged. "My husband and I had a run in with a crazy man who shares the cul-de-sac with us. I'd heard that Mrs. Weaver used to live in our neighborhood, and I was hoping maybe she could shed some light on the relationship between him and his wife."

"That's it?" the detective pressed, holding the paper in one hand and propping her chin on the other. "You called her to ask her opinion on one of you neighbors? You've never met with her or visited her at any time?"

Jessica shook her head, unable to meet Vickerson's gaze. "No."

Laying the paper down on the tabletop, the detective slid it across the wooden surface, stopping it beneath Jessica's nose. "Then how do you explain this?"

Studying the black and white markings on the page, Jessica lifted her gaze. "What's is it?"

"Your fingerprints. Mrs. Nobles. The ones we lifted from Sandy Weaver's living room."

More confusion rushed in. Why would they fingerprint Sandy's living room? "I don't understand. Has something happened to Mrs. Weaver?"

"Her body was found last night, stabbed multiple times."

All the blood drained from Jessica's face. "She's dead?"

The detective opened the folder and pulled several photos from inside. She slid them across the table as she'd done with the paper.

Jessica lowered her gaze to the gruesome images, horror slamming into her gut. Sandy's mutilated body lay sprawled on her living room floor in a pool of her own blood.

"Oh, God." Jessica staggered from her chair, dropped to her knees in front of a small wastebasket by the door, and heaved.

The detective showed no mercy. "I need to know your whereabouts last night, Mrs. Nobles."

Jessica shuddered, another bout of heaves gripping her body. "I stayed at a motel in town," she gasped.

Vickerson knocked on the glass behind her. The door opened a moment later, and a wad of paper towels were thrust beneath Jessica's nose.

She accepted the offering, wiping at her mouth and watery eyes.

"I'll need the name of that motel." Vickerson demanded, suspicion lining her tone. "And why did you lie about knowing Sandy Weaver?".

Jess slowly got to her feet and returned to her chair, careful not to look at the horrific pictures lying before her. "Because, I didn't want you to think I was crazy."

"What I think about your mental status should be the least of your concern, Mrs. Nobles. If I were you, I'd start talking. Sandy Weaver is dead, and the only leads we have to go on seem to involve you."

Swallowing more bile, Jessica pushed the photos across the table out of her field of vision. "I didn't kill her, Detective. You have to believe me."

"Let's start over." Vickerson returned the pictures to the folder. "Why don't you begin by telling me how you came to know Mrs. Weaver."

Jessica spent the next two hours, filling the detective in on everything that had happened since her move to Sparkleberry Hills—ending with, "Sandy asked me to leave, and I did. I haven't spoken to her since."

Vickerson shifted in her chair, crossing her legs at the knee. "What were you doing at the motel last night?"

"My husband and I had been arguing. Things got heated up and I left. I had just come home this morning to get some of my things, when I found you guys there."

"Were you alone at the motel?"

Jessica nodded. "Other than the couple of neighbors I've met, the ex-reporter who worked on the Dayton boy's disappearance and Sandy Weaver, I don't know anyone else here."

"Did you tell anyone about your visit with Sandy Weaver?"

"Steven Ruckle and Melanie Dayton. That's it."

Vickerson jotted the two names down on a piece of paper. "And who are they?"

"Steven is the ex-reporter I mentioned, and Melanie is the mother of the missing boy, Terry Dayton."

The door opened, and an older gentleman stuck his head inside. "We got the search warrant."

Vickerson sent the man a curt nod before scrawling something on a small notepad. "Officers are being sent to search your house and vehicle, Mrs. Nobles. In the meantime, I need to ask you some more questions."

Jessica fought the urge to vomit again. "The keys to the house and my car are in my purse. Please don't let them damage the door to the house."

"Will do."

Chapter Twenty-Six

Owen stood at the window in his office, staring out at the busy traffic beyond. His heart ached with the knowledge that he was quickly losing Jessica. She hadn't come home last night.

The phone on his desk rang, pulling him out of his despairing thoughts. He trailed across the room and snatched up the receiver. "Owen Nobles."

"Hi, Mr. Nobles, it's Marge from across the street."

He'd know her voice anywhere. "Hello, Marge. What can I do for you?"

"I just thought you should know that there are a couple of cops searching your house."

He couldn't have heard her right. Owen had expected an officer to call or stop by with information on the break in, but not to search his home. "Are you sure they're not looking for Jess or me? We were told they might stop by with information about the break in."

"I'm positive," she rushed out. "I walked over there to ask them what was going on. They told me they had a search warrant and asked me to stay out of the way."

Disbelief was instant. Owen tightened his hold on the phone receiver. "Is Jessica there?"

"Her SUV is in the drive. But I didn't see her when they entered the house."

Owen's eyes narrowed. "If she didn't let them in, how did they get inside the house?"

"They had a key."

Thanking Mrs. Hawthorn for notifying him, Owen hung up the phone, grabbed his suit jacket from the back of his chair and sailed from his office.

"I'll be back as soon as I can," he informed his secretary on his way past her desk. "If something urgent arises before I get back, call me on my cell."

She opened her mouth to answer, but Owen only breezed on by. He rushed out the back, unlocked his car, and jumped inside. Why were the police searching his home, and where the hell was Jessica? He didn't know, but he would find out soon enough.

* * * *

Owen arrived home ten minutes later and pulled in behind Jessica's SUV.

He noticed the front door to his house stood open and two patrols cars were parked on the grassy lawn of his yard.

Climbing out, Owen hurried up the drive only to be stopped at the door by the same officer who'd worked the scene the evening before. "Please wait outside, Mr. Nobles. We'll be finished here shortly."

Owen glanced inside in time to see another officer going through Jessica's china cabinet. "Why are you searching our home, and where is my wife?"

"Your wife has been taken into custody for questioning."

Owen threw out his hands. "You couldn't question her here? It was a break in. Nothing was taken."

A small indention appeared between the officer's eyes. "She's a person of interest in a homicide."

"A homicide?" Owen growled. "What homicide?"

"I'm sorry, Mr. Nobles. You'll have to speak with the Banbridge County detective about that. She's at the station with your wife."

Owen realized two things in that moment. He had no idea where the hell Banbridge County was, and Jessica was suspected of homicide.

He rushed back to his car.

Chapter Twenty-Seven

Jessica had never answered so many questions in all her life. Her nerves were shot, and she needed to relieve herself worse than ever before.

"We've confirmed your alibi with Steven Ruckle on your whereabouts yesterday evening. We also confirmed your check in to the motel. Did you leave your room at any time during the night?"

"No," Jessica assured the detective. "I told you, I took an antianxiety pill and went to sleep."

Detective Vickerson jotted down something in her notepad. "How often do you take antianxiety medication?"

"Not very often. I wouldn't have taken one last night had I not been upset about the fight I had with my husband."

"What was the fight about?"

Jessica stomach tightened in dread. "The message left on the wall of our home."

"From the break in," Vickerson murmured, once again writing in her notepad.

"Yes."

The detective looked up, tapping her pen against her chin. "Why would you argue about the writing on the wall?"

What the hell was Jess supposed to say to that? *My husband accused me of being responsible for it?* "I don't know why we fought about it, Detective. I guess both of our nerves were beyond shot by that point."

The questioning went on for another half hour before a tap sounded on the door.

Vickers excused herself and then stepped into the hall, leaving Jessica alone with her anxiety.

They suspected her of killing Sandy Weaver. How was she supposed to clear herself when she was the last one to call or visit the blonde psychic?

Vickers stepped back into the room, a tall, gray-haired gentleman, carrying a briefcase right behind her.

Setting the briefcase on the table, the man announced. "My name is Lucas Hill. I was hired by your husband to represent you."

He then turned his intelligent gaze to Vickerson. "Are you arresting my client?"

The detective shook her head. "Not as of yet."

"Then she has nothing further to say."

Jessica glanced from one to the other.

The attorney gripped Jessica by the elbow and coaxed her to stand. "Let's go, Mrs. Nobles."

Getting to her feet, Jess allowed the attorney to lead her to the door.

"Don't leave town," Vickerson called to Jessica's retreating back. "We'll be in touch."

Jess nodded and stepped into the hall. Neither she or Lucas Hill spoke until they reached the front of the station.

Owen pushed away from the wall. "Are you okay?"

Jessica wanted to run to him, but something in his eyes held her back. "I'm tired, but other than that, yes. I just really want to get out of here."

Owen nodded and then shook the attorney's hand. "Thank you for getting here so fast, Mr. Hill. I'm Owen Nobles, Jessica's husband. We spoke on the phone."

Lucas returned the handshake. "My office is just across the street. If you'll follow me, we'll get everything sorted out in no time."

Releasing the attorney's hand, Owen stepped back and placed his arm around Jessica's shoulders.

She had to admit that it felt good to have her husband to lean on; even if he didn't trust her.

The trio crossed the street and entered a grey, three-story building. They took the elevator to the third floor, following closely behind Hill as he stepped off into the hall and entered a large, extravagant office.

Hill skirted his desk, nodding toward the two leather chairs situated in front of it. "Please, have a seat."

Jessica and Owen sat while the attorney opened a drawer and pulled out some papers.

"My assistant usually handles the paperwork, but she's gone home for the day. I just happened to be here working on a case when your husband called."

Jessica glanced at Owen, noticing the tense set to his jaw. "How did you know I'd been taken to the station?"

"I came home to find the house being searched. One of the officers told me where to find you."

The attorney cleared his throat, bringing Jessica's attention back to him. "I need you to tell me everything. Do you understand? Leave nothing out, no matter how small you think it is."

"I didn't kill that woman," Jessica responded in a weak voice. "I barely even knew her."

Lucas Hill leaned back in his chair. "I spoke with the Sparkleberry Hills police chief. It would seem that they found your fingerprints all over Mrs. Weaver's living room."

Owen's head cranked around in Jessica's direction. "Who is Mrs. Weaver?"

"The psychic I told you about. I went to see her a few days ago to talk with her about the missing Dayton boy."

Owen exhaled loudly. "Were you planning on telling me about this?"

"No," Jessica snapped before pinching the bridge of her nose. "I couldn't tell you, Owen. You would only think I was crazy and demand I see a psychiatrist."

A tense silence ensued and then Owen addressed the attorney. "I'm assuming the psychic is dead?"

"Apparently she was murdered in her own home last night. Your wife is suspected of being the last person to see her alive."

"Jesus," Owen breathed, glancing at Jessica before returning his gaze to the attorney. "What happens now?"

"Once I've heard everything there is to hear, I'll determine if I need to be placed on retainer. But from what I've gathered so far, I think it's safe to say that detective isn't going to stop until your wife is behind bars."

Jessica's heart twisted. "But I didn't do it."

"I'm not here to judge you, Mrs. Nobles. I only need to know what we're up against."

Chapter Twenty-Eight

Owen drove Jessica home, his thoughts a jumbled mess of chaos and disbelief. He couldn't bring himself to look at her for fear she would see the suspicion lurking in his eyes.

The Jessica, Owen had married, would never do something as heinous as what she'd been accused of doing. But he wasn't sure he knew her anymore. The woman sitting in the passenger seat of his car had been a stranger to him since their son's death.

"Why don't you ask me?" Jessica whispered, pulling Owen out of his dark thoughts. "Ask me if I did it."

Owen finally met her gaze. "It wouldn't matter, Jess. You've lied to me so much lately, I'm not sure I would believe anything you told me at this point."

"Then why did you come get me? Why hire an attorney for me?"

He returned his attention to the road. "Because, you're my wife, for better or worse."

"So, I'm an obligation." It wasn't a question.

Owen ground his teeth. "Can't you simply accept the fact that I'm trying to be here for you?"

"First, you accused me of vandalizing our own home, and then came running with an attorney when I'm being questioned for murder. I don't know what to think anymore, Owen. Your mixed signals are driving me crazy."

"You want to talk about crazy? You're seeing things that aren't there, chasing the ghost of a little boy who happened to be the same age as Jacob. How is that for crazy?"

She turned to stare out the window, her silent way of telling him the conversation was over.

Owen drove the rest of the way home in a state of disbelief. His wife had been accused of murder, and he honestly couldn't be sure of her innocence at that point. "I want you to see a doctor."

That brought her head around. "I'm not going back to a psychiatrist, nor am I taking anymore medications, so you can just forget it."

"If you don't go willingly, Jess, I'll have you Baker Acted. I swear to God, I will."

"What the hell is a Baker Act?"

Owen turned into their drive, switched off the car and faced her. "It's a means of providing a person with a mental health evaluation and treatment when required…either on a voluntary or an involuntary basis."

Her mouth fell open. "Involuntary? Meaning you'll have me committed?"

"Evaluated," he quietly corrected, his heart in his throat. "There's a difference."

Tears sprang to her eyes. "To you, maybe. But to me, it's a betrayal."

"What do you expect me to do? Sit around twiddling my thumbs while you continue to spiral out of control? You've left me no choice, Jess."

Jessica opened the car and jumped out. "If you do this, Owen, we are through." The door slammed shut behind her.

Owen remained in the car, unable to move, to take a deep breath. The love of his life was fading away before his eyes. He had to do something quick before she hurt someone else, or worse…herself.

He exited the car, a sick feeling in the pit of his stomach. Had Jessica been responsible for the death of that psychic in Alabama? He didn't want to believe her capable of such a thing, yet the niggling doubt in the far recesses of his mind, told a different story.

He entered the house and made his way to their bedroom to find her packing her things. "I can't let you leave, Jess."

"You can't stop me," she bit out, grabbing items from her top drawer and stuffing them into her suitcase.

Owen pulled his cell phone from his pocket. "Please, Jess. Don't make me do this."

She glanced at him over her shoulder. "If you have me locked up, Owen. You will never see me again. That, I can promise you."

Clenching his teeth to keep from snarling at her, Owen dialed the police department, and asked for a car to be sent to his home.

Jessica kept her back to him, her shoulder's slumping in defeat. She closed the lid to her suitcase and spoke in a voice so soft he could barely understand her. "You break my heart, Owen..."

Chapter Twenty-Nine

"Mrs. Nobles? I need you to take this for me."

Jessica sat in a chair in her small room in the local psychiatric ward and watched as the pretty, young nurse approached, holding a tiny paper cup.

She handed the cup to Jess. "Would you like some water?"

Jess nodded, unable to form words. She was in the Sparkleberry Hills hospital; on the fifth floor which was reserved for mental illness patients. They'd drugged her, entering her room only to administer meds or to help her shower.

"The doctor will be seeing you today," the nurse commented, handing Jessica a cup of water.

Swallowing the pills, Jess took a sip of the water. "How long do I have to stay in here?" She read the nurse's nametag. "Cindy?"

Cindy's gaze softened. "I don't know, Mrs. Nobles. I suppose it all depends on what the doctor decides after your evaluation."

"You mean if he thinks I'm crazy or not," Jess shot back, taking her frustration out on the young nurse.

When Cindy didn't answer, Jessica asked, "Has my husband called?"

"He stopped by earlier to check on you, but you were asleep."

"I don't want to see him," Jessica responded more harshly than she'd intended. "If he comes back, do not allow him in here. Under any circumstances."

Cindy nodding her understanding. "Yes, Mrs. Nobles."

"I need to use the phone."

The nurse glanced toward the door. "We have a phone in the recreation room. I can walk you down if you'd like?"

Jessica pushed to her feet in a haze of drug induced numbness and followed the nurse from the room. They trailed down a short hallway and then turned right into large room with tables scattered throughout.

Dozens of people occupied the area, some sleeping in their chairs while others watched television or paced the room.

A beige colored phone hung on the wall next to a woman sitting at a desk behind a glass window.

"Mrs. Nobles would like to use the phone, Alice," Cindy informed the woman at the desk.

Alice nodded toward the phone. "Local calls only. And keep it short. Calls cut off after ten minutes."

If Jessica had hoped for a little privacy, she was sadly mistaken. The woman behind the glass watched her every move.

Jess picked up the receiver and dialed the only person on the planet that she could trust.

"Ruckle," Steven answered on the third ring.

Relief poured through Jessica. "Steven, it's Jess."

"Hey you. You finally decided to return my call?"

Confused, Jessica mumbled, "You called?"

"Like twenty times." Humor lined his tone. "What's going on?"

"I need to see you, Steven."

He must have picked up on something in her voice. "Is everything okay?"

"No," Jess whispered, tears leaking from the corners of her eyes. "Everything's bad, Steven. Really bad."

"Tell me where you are and I'll come to you."

Jessica's throat closed briefly. It took her a moment to gain enough composure to answer him. "I'm in the Sparkleberry Hills Psyche Ward."

"What?"

"Owen had me Baker Acted last night."

A long pause followed. "I'm on my way." The call ended.

Relieved to know that Steven would be there shortly, Jessica moved to the recreation room to wait.

She took a seat at an empty table, not wishing to engage in conversation with anyone.

Leaning her head back to stare up at the ceiling, Jess let her mind drift to Owen and the closed off look on his face when he'd prevented her from leaving the house last night. He truly thought her crazy.

Her mind drifted back further, back to her wedding day.

Marrying Owen had been the happiest day of Jessica's life aside from Jacob's birth. Owen had been the most handsome, fun-loving man, Jess had ever known.

The two of them had met in college and married not long after graduation. Life couldn't have been more perfect, that is, until their son had been born.

Jacob had quickly become Jessica's entire world. With his mother's dimples and his father's chin, the tiny bundle of joy had been the apple of his parents' eyes.

Losing Jacob had destroyed Jessica, along with her relationship with Owen.

She supposed she didn't blame Owen for distrusting her. Jess had, after all, experienced hallucinations and suicidal thoughts for the better part of the past three years. But she'd gotten stronger, or so she thought. She'd tried so hard to please Owen, had even moved to Florida against her better judgement just to make him happy.

The woman Jessica had seen sitting behind the window stuck her head inside the recreation room. "You have a visitor."

Jessica glanced at the clock on the wall. It had only been a few minutes since she'd spoken with Steven. "Who is it?"

Alice held her gaze. "It's your husband."

"I don't wish to see him."

"Are you sure? He seems really intent on seeing you."

Jessica waved a hand in the air. "I'm positive."

Alice stood there a moment longer, sighed rather loudly and then disappeared from view.

Chapter Thirty

Owen stared down at the short, blonde-haired woman refusing to allow him to see his wife. "Will you at least let her know that I've brought some of her things?"

"She's not permitted to have them, Mr. Nobles. No shoes with strings, no belts, and no jewelry."

It occurred to him that Jessica would be on suicide watch. His stomach tightened in grief. She would never forgive him for having her locked up. No matter how brief her stay might be.

"I understand. Would you mind asking her one more time if she will see me? I won't stay long, and I promise not to upset her."

The lady wearing the nametag *ALICE*, blew out a solemn breath. "I'm sorry, sir, but your wife was very adamant about not wanting to see you. And since she's a patient here, I have to respect her wishes."

Owen could only nod in return. "I'll just try back later."

He left the hospital and drove the short distance to Lucas Hill's office.

"Mr. Hill is with a client at the moment," the attorney's legal assistant informed Owen at once. "If you'd like to have a seat and wait, he should be finished up in the next thirty minutes."

Owen meandered over to a row of brown leather chairs and sat facing the assistant. He wasn't sure exactly what he would say to the attorney once he saw him, he only knew that Jessica needed his help, and Hill was the only person Owen could think of to ask for that help.

Was she responsible for the alleged break in? Owen wondered for the hundredth time.

Moreover, had she killed that psychic? If she had, what could her reasoning have been?

He knew that she'd been seeing things, such as the missing boy in the window. But surely that wouldn't warrant murder. Unless she'd had a mental break and believed Sandy Weaver had been responsible for the Dayton kid's disappearance.

Jessica hadn't been completely sane since Jacob's death. That much Owen knew, yet she couldn't possibly be a killer. *Could she?*

The door to the attorney's office opened, and a woman stepped out, holding the hand of the man at her side. She briefly met Owen's gaze and then trailed off toward the exit door.

"Mr. Nobles?" the attorney murmured, gesturing toward his office. "Come on in."

Owen followed Lucas Hill through the open doorway and took a seat in front of his desk. He waited for Hill to sit as well before getting to the point. "I had Jessica Baker Acted."

Lucas Hill rested his elbows on the desktop and steepled his fingers beneath his chin. "That's not going to help her case. Can you tell me what prompted that decision?"

Owen dropped his head momentarily and then met the attorney's gaze once again. "I think she's had another psychotic break."

The attorney's eyebrows shot up. "Another, as in she has a history of psychotic breaks?"

Feeling guilty for disclosing Jessica's past, Owen shifted in his seat. "She had a temporary break after our son's death a few years ago."

"I'm sorry to hear about your son, Mr. Nobles. My deepest sympathies on your loss."

Owen gave a weak nod. "Thank you."

"What led you to believe your wife had a psychotic break?"

Filling the attorney in on everything that had happened since moving to Florida, Owen ended with, "I think it's strange that the psychic ended up dead shortly after Jessica began hallucinating again. She's seeing things that aren't there and disappearing for hours at a time without answering her phone or text messages."

"She has an alibi for the day the Weaver woman was killed. We're still checking surrounding cameras that can prove she never left the motel later that night. If we can find evidence that she never left that room, she'll be cleared of any suspicion. On another positive note, the murder weapon hasn't been found, which means they have nothing to charge her with."

Owen could only stare at Lucas Hill's face. He hadn't heard much past the alibi Jessica had for earlier that day. "Who is the alibi you mentioned?"

"I'm afraid I can't disclose that information, Mr. Nobles. That's something you'll have to ask your wife."

"But she's not the one who hired you. I am."

Hill leaned back in his chair. "I realize that, but there is a thing called attorney-client privilege that prevents me from disclosing information about the case."

"She's my wife, Mr. Hill. I'm trying to help her. I would never do anything to hurt her case."

The attorney pinned him with a serious look. "You may already have by Baker Acting her."

Chapter Thirty-One

Jessica looked up when Alice poked her head around the corner once more.

"You have another visitor, Mrs. Nobles. A gentleman named Ruckle."

"Please, send him in." Jessica jumped to her feet and rounded the table.

The short blonde nodded and moved out of view.

Seconds later, Steven Ruckle marched into the room, his shoulders back and his eyes reflecting his empathy. "Jesus, Jess."

He wrapped her in a hug, squeezing her hard enough she found it hard to breathe.

Not that she was complaining. It felt good to be held and comforted by someone who wouldn't judge or question her sanity. "Thank you for coming."

With one last gentle squeeze, Steven pulled back but kept his hands on her upper arms. "Of course. What the hell are you doing in this place?"

"Owen felt that I belonged here, I guess. I should never have mentioned what I saw in the upstairs window of the Dayton house."

Steven guided her to a chair, before pulling one up directly in front of her. He took hold of her hands. "Just breathe and start from the beginning."

Once Jessica began talking, she couldn't seem to stop. She told Steven everything that had happened between Owen and her since Jacob's death. "So, you see? He thinks I'm crazy. And rightfully so. I haven't exactly been the model wife for many years now."

"Jessica, listen to me. You are not crazy. Granted, you've been through something that would break even the strongest of people, but you're far from insane. And you damn sure don't belong in this place."

Tears sprang to Jessica's eyes. Steven's words, his faith in her sanity, gave her the strength she needed to get through the ordeal that lay ahead of her. She would be alright. The evidence of that fact shone from Steven's eyes like a beacon in the dark.

"Don't cry," he soothed, wiping away her tears with the pads of his thumbs. "No matter what happens from here on out, know that I believe in you."

Jessica sniffled. "That means more to me than I can say."

"Listen to me, Jessica. I am going to do everything in my power to get you out of here. Worst case scenario, you have to stay for a couple of days. They can't legally hold you here for more than seventy-two-hours, and you've already been here for twenty-four. Right?"

At her nod, he continued, "I have a guest house you can stay in until you and your husband can work things out."

Jessica shook her head. "I can't ask you to do that."

"You didn't ask. I offered. Now, next question. Did you kill Sandy Weaver?"

"No," Jess wheezed, her heart in her throat. "I could never have done such a thing."

Steven reached for her hands once again. "Easy. I just wanted to look into your eyes when you told me. I believe you, Jessica, and I'll do everything I can to help you clear your name."

Jess studied his handsome face. "Why are you helping me?"

"Because I covered this case for over three years. A lot of strange things went on that were never investigated. I believe you're being set up."

"But why? Why would someone want to murder poor Sandy Weaver, and then make it look as if I did it?"

A muscle tightened in Steven's jaw. "I believe you pose a threat to the person responsible for Terry Dayton's disappearance. We just have to figure out who that individual is."

"I really did see Terry in that upstairs window." Jessica watched Steven's eyes for any signs of doubt, but he only stared back at her in open curiosity.

"If you think you saw Terry's ghost, then I believe you."

Running a hand down her face, Jessica whispered, "I don't think I saw him. I know I did."

"Good enough for me." He got to his feet.

Jess stood as well. "Where are you going?"

"To see if I can speak with the doctor on staff. Hopefully, we can get you out of here sooner rather than later."

Jessica hoped so too.

* * * *

Steven returned a half hour later, tension obvious in his every step. Running a hand through his hair, he approached Jessica. "There's nothing I can do to get you out of here before the seventy-two-hour evaluation period is up. Especially since you're married, and your husband was the one who had you Baker Acted."

Jessica hated Owen in that moment. "So I'm stuck here?"

"I'm afraid so. But the good news is, you'll be free in two more days. In the meantime, I'll be working on clearing your name."

"How are you going to do that?"

"By going over old evidence in the Dayton case. There has to be something we overlooked that will lead us in the direction of the person responsible for Terry's disappearance. Once I get an idea of who that might be, I'll be one step closer to figuring out who is doing this to you."

Jessica remained in her seat, her legs too weak to stand. She gazed up into Steven's determined face. "I don't know how to thank you for everything you've done for me."

"I haven't done anything yet, but I will." With that, he turned and left.

Chapter Thirty-Two

Jessica returned to her hospital room, a sinking feeling in her gut as she heard the door lock behind her.

She moved to sit on the side of her bed, her stomach in knots and her head pounding with a tension headache.

Jess wasn't sure how long she sat there before the door opened and Cindy appeared. "Come with me."

"Where am I going?" Jess stood and followed Cindy into the hallway.

"To see Doctor Roberts."

The walk to the room where the doctor waited was spent with Jessica battling her nerves. Cindy moved along quietly before stopping outside a closed door, knocking softly and then pushing it open.

Jessica stepped inside, her gaze zeroing in on a man sitting in a chair near the center of the room.

He waved toward the chair in front of him, without looking up. "Have a seat Mrs. Nobles."

The door clicked softly shut with Cindy's departure.

Jessica lowered herself into the chair and waited for him to finish reading the chart he held in his hand.

He eventually closed the chart and lifted his head. "You can relax, Mrs. Nobles. I'm not going to bite you."

She noticed that he had kind eyes. "It's hard for me to relax, Doctor. I'm not even supposed to be here."

Leaning back and crossing his legs at the knee, the doctor murmured, "Fair enough.

Then why don't you begin by telling me how you came to be here?"

"My husband had me Baker Acted. I didn't even know such a thing existed."

The doctor pulled a pair of glasses from his shirt pocket, put them on and opened her chart once more. "Your husband stated that you've been hallucinating. He also believes you staged a break in at your residence."

Anger surfaced, but Jess breathed her way through it. The last thing she needed was to lose her cool in front of the doctor. He alone held the power to prove her not insane. "Just because a person suspects you of something, doesn't make it the truth."

"I see. Did you stage the break in at your residence?"

Jessica shook her head. "Of course not. Why would I do such a thing?"

"You tell me."

It quickly became obvious to Jess that the doctor doubted her innocence in staging the home invasion. "Look. I get it that you deal with mental illness on a daily basis. I also understand why you would be suspicious of my involvement in the break in. But I'm telling you, I did not do it."

"Tell me about the hallucinations."

Here it comes, Jess thought, wondering how to respond. "I haven't been hallucinating. I simply thought I saw something in a window of the abandoned house next door to us. Apparently, it was the glare of the streetlight."

The doctor flipped a page up on the chart he held. "You didn't tell you husband that you saw a boy…wearing a striped T-shirt? A boy with long, dark hair that had come up missing in that very house thirteen years before?"

"No," Jessica lied, holding the doctor's gaze. "I mentioned to him that a boy disappeared while living in that house, but I never said I saw him. That child would be twenty years old now."

Doctor Roberts closed the chart and pushed his glasses up on his nose. "If I'm expected to help you, Mrs. Nobles, I'm going to need complete honesty."

"I am being honest!"

Leaning back once more, the doctor folded his hands on top of Jessica's chart. "I read the police report. You told Detective Vickerson that you saw Terry Dayton's ghost in that abandoned house. You also stated that you'd gone to visit the psychic to show her a painting of the boy in a shallow grave — a painting you don't recall creating. Can you explain that to me?"

She couldn't explain any of it, so instead of answering, she simply shrugged.

"From what I've observed along with your husband's accounting and the police report, I'm not so sure you're not experiencing Organic Psychosis. It's a—"

"I know what it is," Jess bit out, cutting off the rest of his words. "But you're wrong. I'm thinking clearer than I have in years."

"I'd like to keep you here for a couple more days." He held up a hand when she would have interrupted. "Strictly for observation purposes. I would also like to run a few tests and try you on a different medication than you've had in the past."

Jessica fought back new tears. "I don't need to be medicated, Doctor Roberts. I'm telling you, I'm fine."

The doctor set Jessica's chart on the corner of his desk, uncrossed his legs, and leaned forward with his elbows resting on his knees.

"I'd like to believe that, Mrs. Nobles, but it's my job to ensure your safety."

Gaining his feet, the doctor stared down at Jess before offering her his hand.

She stood without assistance and turned for the door. "You can't keep me in here indefinitely."

"You're right about that," he responded as she gripped the doorknob. "But a judge can. If you don't help me to help you, you're tying my hands if your case ends up in a court of law."

Jessica paused before jerking the door open and nearly running into Cindy.

The nurse took hold of her elbow. "Let's return to your room."

Jessica's bottom lip trembled, but she bit down on it to prevent herself from crying. She merely nodded, allowing the nurse to escort her back to her temporary prison.

Chapter Thirty-Three

"Here are the things you had when you arrived." Alice slid a white hospital bag through the opening at the bottom of the glass she sat behind.

Jessica accepted the bag with a terse nod and turned to face Steven who waited by the door. "I'm ready."

He relieved her of the bag she held, opened the door, and stepped back to allow her to pass.

She didn't speak again until they reached the elevators. "Thank you for picking me up."

"Not a problem." He pressed the elevator button. "Besides, I couldn't very well leave you to your own devices. God knows where you'd end up next."

Jessica smiled for the first time in days. She seemed to do that a lot when in Steven's presence. "Are you afraid I might show up at your job and parade naked through the halls, shouting your name?"

"More like afraid you won't," he quipped.

Stepping onto the elevator, Jessica sobered. "According to the doctor back there, your fears are warranted."

"Yeah, well what does he know?" Steven stepped in behind her and pressed the button to the bottom floor.

Jessica grew quiet for a moment, studying Steven's profile. "Why are you really helping me?"

"I've already told you...I believe you."

"I wouldn't believe me if I were in your shoes."

He glanced down at her. "I guess it's a good thing you're not in my shoes, isn't it?"

"Yeah."

The elevator came to a sudden stop, and the door slid open to reveal a very disheveled, very surprised looking Owen.

He took a step back, his gaze zeroing in on the hospital bag Steven held before shifting back to Jessica. "What's going on here?"

Jessica folded her arms across her chest and stepped up next to Steven. "I could ask you the same question. What are you doing here, Owen?"

"I was coming to give you a ride home."

Taking hold of Steven's arm, Jessica lifted her chin. "I have a ride. Now, if you'll excuse us."

Owen's jaw visibly tightened. His eyes narrowed, and his gaze swung in Steven's direction. "Who the hell are you?"

"You don't get to ask that," Jessica snapped before Steven had a chance to respond.

"I'm your husband, Jess. I believe I have a right to know who the man is that my wife is clinging so tightly to."

Jessica had to force her teeth apart to answer him. "You gave up any rights you had to me when you put me in this place."

Defeat took up residence in Owen's eyes. "I did what I thought was best. If you would just talk to me, I—"

"Move!" Jessica snapped, holding her husband's gaze.

He hesitated a moment longer and then stepped to the side.

Jessica clung tightly to Steven's arm as he led her from the elevator and down the hall to the exit.

"I apologize for that," she rushed out the second they cleared the hospital doors. "Had I known we would run into him, I would have suggested we take the stairs."

Steven jerked his chin toward a row of vehicles not far from the hospital entrance. "I'm parked over there. And you have nothing to apologize for. You couldn't have known he'd be there."

Jessica made her way to Steven's car and opened the passenger side door. "No, but I should have guessed he would."

Steven got behind the wheel and inserted the key into the ignition. "Where would you like to go?"

"Anywhere but home."

The car started on cue. "Anywhere, it is."

Jessica snapped on her seatbelt, relieved to feel the air conditioning blowing on her overheated face. She turned to stare out the window, watching as the hospital slowly disappeared from view.

It took her a second to realize Steven was speaking to her. She twisted her head around to face him. "I'm sorry, what?"

"I asked if you were hungry."

She wasn't, but she couldn't recall the last time she'd eaten anything. "A little. Whatever you want is fine by me. I'm not particular."

"My kind of woman," Steven teased, pulling onto the main road. He quickly sped toward the busy intersection in the distance, leaving Owen and that dreadful hospital far behind.

Chapter Thirty-Four

Jessica finished everything on her plate and was working on dessert when Steven leaned back in his chair with a groan.

"I can't eat another bite," he pointed out unnecessarily, nodding toward his now empty dish.

Jess picked up her napkin and wiped her mouth. "That was delicious. I had no idea how hungry I actually was until I took the first bite."

"I've always been a huge fan of Mexican food." Steven took a drink of his water before continuing. "It's second only to sushi in my book."

"Sushi is my favorite as well." She picked up her sweating water glass, watching the small ice-cubes float around inside. "I have to figure out a way to clear my name."

Returning his glass to the table, Steven held her gaze for long moments. "I agree. We just need to figure out where to start."

"I think we should begin with Eustice Martin."

Steven didn't blink. "Easy enough. We can go back to my office and pull up everything I had on him from years ago. But that's only going to get us so far. We need to find out what was used to write the words on your wall, and also see if we can locate Sandy Weaver's murder weapon."

"You think Eustice would keep the murder weapon just lying around? Assuming he did it, that is."

With a shrug, Steven dug his wallet out of his pocket. "Hard to say, but since he's not a suspect, I doubt he'd go out of his way to hide it. Especially if he intends to use it to frame you."

Jessica's heart summersaulted. "Frame me?"

"If he killed Sandy Weaver, it was to make it look as if you did it. Otherwise, what would be the point in killing her?"

"Maybe because she was a psychic, and he worried she might see something?"

Steven shook his head. "Doubtful. If she hadn't seen anything before now or turned him in after thirteen years for threatening her, he probably didn't consider her a threat. No, I'm thinking someone killed her to make you look guilty."

Jessica's food settled like a brick in her stomach. "He's the only one who had motive to kill her."

"Perhaps, but we don't know that for certain. We have no idea what all she was involved in. She could have been killed for reasons that had nothing to do with you, and you just happened to be in the wrong place at the wrong time."

"Then they might never know who killed her. Which will always leave me their prime suspect."

Laying enough money on the table to cover the bill and the tip, Steven pushed his chair back and stood. "Stop worrying, Jess. As long as they don't have a murder weapon, that's all you'll ever be to them...a suspect."

Jess didn't want to be suspected of killing Sandy any more than she wanted Owen suspecting her of breaking into their home and leaving those words on the wall. "I just want this all to end, Steven."

"I know you do." He offered her his hand, which she readily accepted.

How was it that a man she barely knew could make her feel safe and protected, while her own husband—the man who'd vowed to cherish her until death do they part—could betray her?

Steven's warm palm closed around her hand, his thumb grazing softly over her knuckles. "I promise you, we'll get to the bottom of this."

"I wish I had your optimism."

Another swipe of his thumb across her knuckles. "I wasn't always so optimistic. It took years of digging, researching, and bloodhounding to develop that particular skill. I've learned that the truth can always be found if you dig deep enough."

Once they reached the car, Steven released his hold on her hand and unlocked her door. "You're welcome to the guesthouse if you need a place to crash for a while."

"I couldn't possibly impose." She ducked into the passenger seat.

Steven closed her door, skirted the front of the car and got behind the wheel. "It's no imposition. In fact, stay as long as you'd like."

* * * *

Jessica wasn't sure how she felt about staying in Steven's guesthouse, but the alternative would be a motel room without transportation. She highly doubted that Owen would allow her access to her car, especially after her earlier stunt in the elevator.

The look in Owen's eyes had secretly torn at Jessica's heart, yet for the life of her, she couldn't understand why. He didn't trust her, and he'd gone so far as to accuse her of staging the break in. Not to mention having her Baker Acted.

She moved around the small guesthouse, admiring the furnishings. Steven had excellent taste, she noted, running the palm of her hand along the back of a red loveseat. Owen had never taken an interest in their home's décor, leaving all the furnishing decisions to Jess.

Why was she comparing the two men as if they were in some sort of competition? Perhaps it had to do with the fact that Steven trusted her. He didn't think her crazy or unhinged, and if he did, he hid it well.

A knock sounded on the door, startling Jess.

"It's open," she called, knowing without looking that it would be Steven.

He stepped into the room, holding a thick folder in his arms. "I thought we could start here."

Jessica nodded toward the folder. "What is that?"

"Some of the notes I took when I was covering the Dayton boy's disappearance."

Steven set the folder down on a small coffee table and took a seat on the red loveseat. Taking hold of the corner, he flipped the folder open. "Have a look."

Ambling over to sit next to him, Jess plucked up the first paper in the thick stack. It happened to be a picture of the drunk, blond man she'd had a confrontation with not long ago. "This is Dale Schroder. Why would you have a photo of him, was he a suspect?"

"No, but he had no alibi for the night Terry went missing. He also refused to cooperate during the investigation."

Jess studied the picture closely, noticing a certain emptiness to Dale's eyes. "He looks like your typical weirdo to me."

Steven nodded. "I agree, but being a weirdo doesn't make you a killer. Besides, he'd just lost his wife to cancer a couple months before Terry disappeared. That could have something to do with his lack of cooperation."

Jessica could relate. She'd completely lost interest in anything and everything when Jacob died.

She laid the photo aside and picked up the next paper in the stack. "This is Eustice Martin's criminal history." She read through the charges, taking in everything from two DUI's to his murder charge. There were also numerous domestic abuse allegations, but he'd never been arrested for any of them.

"His wife never pressed charges," Steven pointed out unnecessarily. "I tried talking to her on several different occasions, but she remained tight-lipped. Out of fear, I'm sure."

Jessica spent the next half-hour, going through the folder. "What about Terry's parents? Did they have anyone in particular they suspected?"

Steven blew out a breath and leaned back against the couch. "I tried dozens of times to interview them, but Melanie was inconsolable. The one time I did manage to sit down with her, she cried through the questioning."

"So she wasn't much help," Jessica murmured. "I can sympathize. It took me three years to be able to speak Jacob's name without breaking down. I still get choked up if I allow myself to dwell on him."

"I'm sorry, Jess."

Uncomfortable with the attention now on her, Jess changed the subject. "What about Terry's father?"

"Jasper Dayton? What about him?"

Jess shifted on her seat to face Steven. "Did he have any helpful information?"

"Not really. He was pretty distraught as well. Although, he did demand the police look into Mr. Hawthorn. He claimed he'd caught the man looking into his windows with a pair of binoculars on more than one occasion."

Jessica's mouth dropped open. "Benny Hawthorn...a peeping Tom?"

"So, I was told. Although, I never found any evidence to validate the accusation. No police report had been filed."

Jess quickly stood. "I want to speak to the Daytons."

"Didn't you already attempt that? As I recall, it didn't go over too well."

Staring down into Steven's calm expression, Jessica admitted, "You're right, it didn't go over well at all. But I have to try. Maybe one of them will remember something that will help me figure out who is doing this to me and why they want me gone."

Steven ran a hand down his face and then pushed to his feet. "Okay, but I'm going with you."

"No," Jess blurted a little harsher than she'd intended. She took a deep breath, softening her gaze. "It's just that...I think it will look as if I brought reinforcement. Melanie would probably go on the defensive. Let me try this on my own."

Steven watched Jess from his great height for several heartbeats before pulling a set of keys from his pants pocket. "Take my car. A cab would be far too expensive."

Jess accepted the keys. "Are you sure?"

"Of course. Drive safely."

Chapter Thirty-Five

Jessica pulled up next to the curb in front of Jasper and Melanie Dayton's pale, stucco home. Her hands shook so badly, she could barely switch off the engine.

A tall, handsome man with short, brown hair, exited the garage holding a bucket and what appeared to be a pile of rags.

The man dropped the rags into the bucket, brought his hand up to shield his eyes from the sun and then set the bucket next to a white truck that read, *DAYTON'S CONSTRUCTION* on the side.

Jessica climbed from the car, hurried up the drive, and cleared her throat. "Mr. Dayton?"

He nodded, slowly lowered his hand from above his eyes, and then sauntered over, stopping a few feet in front of Jessica. "What can I do for you?"

"My name is Jessica Nobles." Jess extended her hand in greeting. "I'm sorry to drop in unannounced this way, but I was wondering if I could ask you a few questions about your son's disappearance?"

Jasper's gaze became guarded. He accepted Jessica's palm. "My wife told me about your recent visit. She won't be happy about you showing up again."

"I know, and I'm really sorry, but I have nowhere else to turn. I need your help, Mr. Dayton."

Releasing his hold on her hand, Jasper glanced toward the house. "Help with what?"

"Someone is trying to make it look like I'm guilty of crimes I didn't commit, and I have a feeling it has something to do with me looking into your son's disappearance. I believe someone in my neighborhood is behind it."

Jasper studied her for a moment longer. "We can talk inside."

Jessica hated like hell to follow him into that garage but follow him she did.

"Mel?" Jasper called out as he stepped into an immaculately clean kitchen.

Melanie Dayton rounded the corner holding a phone in one hand and an envelope in the other. Jess assumed she'd been paying bills.

"What is *she* doing here?" Melanie paled, her stance becoming rigid.

Jasper held up his hands in a defensive manner. "She says she needs our help. I invited her inside, Mel. I figured it wouldn't hurt to hear her out."

Melanie's shoulders remained stiff. She set the phone and envelope on the kitchen counter and crossed her arms over her chest. "If you've come here with more insanity about seeing ghosts, I'll call the police and have you locked up for harassment."

Jessica's heart lurched. The last thing she wanted or needed was for the authorities to be called. She took a hesitant step forward. "I didn't come about that. Please, just hear me out."

Though, Melanie relaxed somewhat, her expression remained tense. "Make it quick."

Jasper intervened. "Let's all move to the den and have a seat."

Thankful for Jasper's intervention, Jessica sent him a grateful look and preceded them into the front room. She took a seat on the same sofa she'd sat on during her last visit to the Dayton's.

Melanie perched on the edge of a high-backed chair, while Jasper took up residence behind her. He rested his hands on his wife's shoulders. "Would you care for something to drink?"

Jessica shook her head. "No, thank you."

"Very well," Jasper continued. "Why don't you start by telling us what this is all about?"

Taking a nervous breath, Jessica filled them in on everything that had happened since moving into the house on Meadowbrook Circle, ending with, "I can't imagine why anyone would want to break into my home and leave such a message on my wall, let alone kill poor Sandy Weaver."

Melanie had paled even more during Jessica's recanting of the last week. "The psychic died the day after you visited me?"

"Yes," Jess whispered, clasping her hands together in her lap.

Clearing her throat, Melanie asked, "How can we be sure that you didn't do it?"

"You can't. Actually, no one can. Other than the fact that I had no motive and barely knew the woman, I have nothing but my word that I'm innocent."

Jasper moved away from his wife and lowered his weight into a chair across from the sofa that Jessica sat on. "What is it that you want from us?"

A tiny spark of hope soared inside Jess. Jasper believed her. She could see it in his eyes. "Your help in proving my innocence."

"I don't see how we can be of any help," Jasper responded in a quiet tone.

Jessica sent him a pleading look. "If there is anything at all you can remember about your son's investigation that might shed some light on why this is happening to me, that would be a good start."

Jasper leaned forward, resting his elbows on his knees. A faraway look entered his eyes.

"I know they investigated Eustice Martin, his wife Gerri, the Hawthorns, Sandy Weaver and Dale Schroder. They also questioned the Peewee football coach at the school my son attended and the registered sex offender who lived two blocks from us at the time."

That was the first Jess had heard of the sex offender and the Peewee football coach. "Do you happen to remember their names?"

Jasper rattled off the two men's names and then pinned Jessica with a serious stare. "Melanie told me that you thought you saw Terry in the upstairs window of our old house."

Melanie jumped to her feet and faced her husband. "I asked you not to bring that up again. Clearly this woman is insane, yet you invite her into our home and entertain her preposterous ideas of being framed?"

"I know what it sounds like," Jessica interjected, drawing Melanie's attention back to her. "But I swear to you, I'm telling the truth. If you don't believe me, you can call Steven Ruckle. He'll tell you I'm not making this up."

"Steven Ruckle?" Melanie and Jasper simultaneously chorused.

Jessica looked from one to the other before focusing on a now standing Jasper. "You know Steven?"

"Unfortunately. The question is, how do you know him?"

"He was the reporter that covered your son's disappearance. I found him through an internet search."

A harsh laugh escaped Jasper. "Ruckle was more than some reporter who covered my son's story. He was my wife's lover."

All the blood drained from Jessica's face. She couldn't have heard him right.

Shifting her stunned gaze to Melanie, Jessica swallowed around her disbelief. "Y-you...I..."

Melanie smoothed her palms down the front of her skirt. "Steven and I...became close during my employment for The Daily Sun."

"Which, in my opinion," Jasper ground out, "is the reason why he asked to be assigned to cover Terry's disappearance. So that he could be closer to my wife."

Swinging around to face her husband, Melanie's hands flew to her hips. "Steven may have been a lot of things, but an opportunist he wasn't. He would have never used our personal tragedy to his advantage like that."

"Still defending him after all this time." Jasper spun on his heel and headed toward the front door. "I need some air."

Once the door shut behind her husband, Melanie returned to her seat. "I'm sorry you had to see that. Steven Ruckle is still a sore subject around here. Even though our...friendship was more than sixteen years ago."

Jessica remained quiet, her mind still reeling with the knowledge that Melanie Dayton had been intimately involved with Steven. How could he have kept that piece of information from her? "I'm not here to judge you, Mrs. Dayton. I'm just hoping that you can help me figure out who would possibly want me gone bad enough to break in my home and to make it look as if I killed Sandy Weaver."

The sound of a vehicle revved to life and then slowly faded as it moved away from the house. Obviously, Jasper had taken off.

Melanie tucked her pretty blonde hair behind her ears and glanced toward the door before returning her gaze to Jessica. "I have no idea who would do such a thing. But from what I remember of Sandy Weaver, she was a paranoid fruit cake who claimed to have seen my son buried in a shallow grave. With that being said, I'm sorry she died the way she did. No one deserves such a horrible death."

"Then you must think I'm crazy as well," Jessica whispered, remembering the last conversation she'd had with Melanie.

"Regardless of what I think, I know that you lost a child a few years ago...and for that, I am deeply sorry. If anyone understands the pain you've experienced, I do."

Jessica fought back the tears that threatened and decided not to reiterate her encounters with Terry's ghost to Melanie—at least for the time being. Right then, she needed the Daytons' help in clearing her name. "Tell me about your relationship with Eustice Martin."

Chapter Thirty-Six

Owen Nobles paced the confines of his living room, heartsick and more than a little pissed off. Not only had Jessica pulled away from him both emotionally and physically, but she'd obviously replaced him with another man.

No, Jessica wouldn't cheat on him, he thought, making another pass across the hardwood floor. No matter how insane her current mental state happened to be.

He glanced at the clock on the wall, realizing it was nearing midnight. Where had Jessica gone? Her car remained in the driveway and according to their bank records, she hadn't used her debit card since leaving the hospital.

The sudden sounds of sirens coming up the road jerked Owen out of his anxiety-induced thoughts. He moved to one of the windows at the front of his house and watched as several police cars whipped into Eustice Martin's drive.

"What the hell?"

Four officers descended from the vehicles, weapons drawn.

Owen could only watch in amazement as the officers ducked low and stealthily slinked forward.

Two of the officers circled toward the back of the Martins' home while the others made their way to the front of the house.

The door abruptly opened to reveal a sobbing Mrs. Martin. She staggered outside, her voice barely audible from the distance. She lifted an arm and pointed behind her.

One of the officers, took hold of her elbow and guided her to his patrol car as his partner cautiously entered the Martins' home.

Owen rushed to the door, curiosity forcing him outside. He tightened the belt of his robe, watching as the officers soon gathered in the Martins' front yard, their weapons holstered.

The rest of the neighborhood began filing onto the street, obviously curious about the commotion taking place in their midst.

Mrs. Hawthorn quickly ambled across the cul-de-sac, the curlers on her head, bouncing with every step she took. She stopped at the edge of Owen's porch.

"What's going on over there?" She nodded toward the Martins' house.

"I don't know, but Mrs. Martin is in the backseat of the police car. I haven't seen Eustice, yet."

"Maybe she finally had enough," Marge sniffed, crossing her arms over her ample chest, "and took a frying pan to his skull."

Owen lifted an eyebrow and glanced down at his nosy neighbor dressed in a dark-green robe.

"Well," she stated defensively, "that's what I would do."

Marge suddenly glanced toward Owen's open front door. "Is Jessica sleeping?"

Owen reached back and pulled the door closed. "She's not home."

"Really? Her car is in the drive."

Grinding his teeth, Owen merely nodded and kept his gaze on the officers standing around in the Martins' front yard.

A black van turned onto Meadowbrook Circle, carefully maneuvering past the crowds of onlookers before pulling up next to the patrol cars. Owen noticed the words CRIME SCENE INVESTGATION on the side of the van.

"Oh, my God." Marge's hand flew to her throat. "That can only mean one thing."

Owen met the older woman's gaze. "Apparently Eustice is dead."

Marge's face turned sheet white. "Geraldine killed Eustice?"

"Looks that way." Owen glanced at Gerri's silhouette, perched in the backseat of that patrol car. Though he couldn't make out her features in the flashing red lights, he could tell that her shoulders slumped forward. In defeat or relief, he couldn't be sure.

Marge abruptly fled Owen's porch; her dark green robe flying out behind her as she ran toward the street where her husband now stood.

Owen could see her pointing toward the Martins' place, her curlers bouncing around on her head with every word she uttered.

Returning his attention to the crime scene, Owen watched two individuals climb from the CSI van, holding some sort of black boxes in their hands. They trailed up to the front door and then disappeared inside.

The officers on scene abruptly dispersed in different directions. Some strode off down the street to question the onlookers, while one made his way toward Owen.

"Good evening," Owen greeted as the officer stepped up onto the porch. "What's going on over there?"

Pulling a small pad and pen from his shirt pocket, the officer sent Owen a curt nod. "Evening, Mister?"

"Nobles. Owen Nobles."

The officer scratched down some words and then peered closely at Owen. "Did you happen to see or hear anything suspicious coming from next door this evening?"

Owen shook his head. "No, but I haven't been up long. What happened over there?"

"We have a possible homicide. Are you sure you didn't notice anything unusual?"

So, Owen's suspicions were true. Eustice was dead. "Like I told you, I've been asleep. I had just got up to get a drink when I heard the sirens."

The officer glanced at the vehicles in the drive. "Do you live here alone. Mr. Nobles?"

"No. My wife Jessica lives here as well."

"Where is she? I'd like to ask her a few questions."

Owen stared at the cop without blinking. "I have no idea."

Lowering his notepad, the officer sent Owen a questioning look. "You don't know where your wife is?"

"I don't. We're going through a rough patch right now. She didn't come home tonight."

The officer lifted the notepad once more. "Spell her name for me."

Owen did as he'd been asked. "I don't see what my wife has to do with any of this. She wasn't even home when it happened."

"I never said when the incident occurred, Mr. Nobles. I also didn't indicate that your wife had anything to do with it. I'm simply making inquiries."

And on it went. Owen stood on his porch, answering the dozens of questions being thrown at him before the officer flipped his notepad closed and returned it to his shirt pocket.

"If we need anything else from you, we'll be in touch."

Owen didn't respond. He held completely still, watching as the officer sauntered across his yard toward the Martins' property.

Why had the cop questioned him about Jessica's whereabouts? She hadn't been home in days. She couldn't possibly know anything about Eustice Martin's murder. And apparently, that's exactly what they were calling it...murder.

Chapter Thirty-Seven

Jessica woke to the smell of coffee. She quickly sat up, surprised to find Steven sitting in a chair across from the small, red loveseat she'd slept on.

He sent her a smile, nodding toward a steaming cup of coffee perched on the table between them. "Good morning."

More than a little shaken by his unexpected presence, Jessica sat up and pushed her hair from her eyes. "You startled me."

"Sorry. The door was open when I arrived this morning. I assumed it was for my benefit."

Jessica glanced toward the door in question. "I don't even remember coming in last night. I was so exhausted, I obviously didn't make it to the bed."

"Were you drinking?"

She had been. Jess had left the Daytons' and stopped at a local sports bar to grab a bite to eat. She hadn't intended to order alcohol, it had just sort of happened. "I had a couple of drinks."

"A couple, huh? You're damn lucky you didn't get a DUI."

Picking up the cup of coffee, Jess took a small sip, nearly groaning aloud as the deliciously hot liquid slid down her throat. "I had a long talk with the Daytons."

She watched him closely for any sign of interest but saw only mild curiosity. "Did you find the answers you sought?"

"Not really. How come you didn't tell me you had an affair with Melanie Dayton?"

Steven leaned back in his chair. "I didn't see any relevance in it. Besides, that was over sixteen years ago. It has nothing to do with what's going on now."

"Maybe not, but you still could have told me." Jess hated the jealousy that echoed in her voice. Surely to God, she wasn't jealous of Steven's history with Melanie, was she?

"I'm not sure why it matters, but I apologize. I should have told you."

Jessica blew out a shaky breath. "It's fine. I just thought that since we've become friends..."

"Friends," Steven repeated in a soft tone. "Is that what this is?"

Suddenly nervous, Jessica changed the subject. "Apparently Jasper Dayton still harbors some anger and resentment toward you."

"I can't say that I blame him." Steven ran a hand through his hair. "I reckon it's a good thing I didn't go with you to see them."

Jessica took another sip of her coffee. "I suppose not. After your name was mentioned, Jasper left out of there in a hurry."

Steven couldn't hide his surprise. "You would think he'd have let it go after all this time."

Jessica changed the subject, not wanting to discuss Steven's past with the Daytons at the moment. "I need clothes."

"I can take you by your place to pick up some things."

Glancing at the clock on the wall, Jessica nodded. "Owen will be leaving for work in a few minutes. I damn sure don't want to run into him right now."

Steven tilted his head to the side. "What are you going to do about him?"

"Owen?"

At Steven's nod, she answered. "I don't know. There's not a whole hell of a lot I can do until my name is cleared of Sandy's murder."

"You don't have to prove your innocence, Jessica. The state has the burden of proving your guilt. And since you're not guilty, you have nothing to worry about."

Jessica would love for that to be true. "Someone has gone to a whole hell of a lot of trouble of making me look guilty, Steven. I'm going to worry until I find out who's doing this to me."

"Fair enough." He pushed to his feet. "Finish your coffee and I'll take you to your house to grab some clothes."

* * * *

The first thing Jessica noticed as Steven turned onto Meadowbrook Circle was the number of police cars parked in the Martins' driveway. "What the hell?"

Steven pulled in behind Jessica's car and switched off the engine. "Something big must have happened at your neighbor's place."

Jessica opened her car door and slowly got out.

Yellow crime scene tape surrounded the Martins' brick home, and several uniformed officers milled about.

A tall, gray-haired man, wearing khakis and a green polo shirt, looked up from the officer he spoke to and marched off in Jessica's direction. "Mrs. Nobles?"

Jessica stilled, recognizing the man as the chief of police.

He came to a stop in front of her and extended his hand. "I'm Gary Randall, chief of police. We met at the station a few days ago."

Accepting his outstretched palm, Jessica attempted a smile she didn't feel. "I remember. What's going on?"

"Would you mind if I came inside and asked you a few questions?"

Jessica glanced at Steven to find him standing calmly by the front of the car before she returned her attention to the police chief. "Sure, if you don't mind Mr. Ruckle joining us."

Gary glanced in Steven's direction. "Not a problem."

The three of them made their way up the drive to the porch. Jessica unlocked the door and waved the two men inside.

"May I offer you something to drink?" She kept her gaze on Chief Randall as she spoke.

"No thank you. I won't take up too much of your time."

Randall and Steven took a seat on the sofa while Jessica lowered herself into a recliner, facing them.

"What can I do for you?" Jessica murmured, getting right to the point.

"I'm not sure if you know what's going on next door, but Eustice Martin was murdered last night."

Nausea flooded Jessica's gut. She sat forward on the recliner, fighting the urge to vomit. "Eustice is dead?"

Randall stared at her for long moments before answering. "One of the officers on scene last night spoke with your husband. Do you mind telling me where you were between nine and eleven pm last night?"

"She was with me," Steven rumbled before Jessica could answer.

Her gaze flew to Steven's calm and serene face.

Randall pulled a small pad from his shirt pocket, followed by a pen. "And you are?"

"Steven Ruckle. I'm a friend of Jessica's."

"I see." Randall scribbled something in his note pad. "And how long have you known Mrs. Nobles?"

Steven didn't bat an eye at the police chief's questions. "A few weeks now."

"And the nature of your relationship?" Randall persisted, suspicion lurking in his intelligent eyes.

"How is my relationship with Mrs. Nobles relevant to what happened to Eustice Martin?"

Randall continued to write. "I'm simply trying to establish motive and rule out unnecessary suspects. So, I'll ask again, what—"

"We're friends," Jessica interrupted, drawing Randall's attention back to her. "Just friends."

Jessica sat glued to that recliner answering Randall's many questions. She didn't dare look at Steven for fear of what she'd see in his eyes. He had to be wondering about her whereabouts last night. But then, why cover for her?

Randall stood and handed Jessica a card. "If you think of anything that might be of help, give me a call."

Accepting the police chief's card, Jessica promised to do just that. She followed him to the door. "How is Mrs. Martin holding up?"

"She's in shock as you can imagine. She's the one who found her husband's body."

Jessica swallowed with some difficulty. "How did he die?"

"His throat was cut."

The floor titled beneath Jessica's feet. Someone had cut Eustice Martin's throat. It couldn't have been his wife, she feared Eustice too much to attempt such a thing, not to mention, he could have overpowered her. No, it had to have been someone strong enough to pull it off.

Standing in the open doorway, Jess waited for the police chief to make it back to his car before slowly turning to face Steven. "Why did you lie about being with me last night?"

He stared back at her, his gaze unreadable. "Would you rather I threw you under the bus?"

"No, but my whereabouts could have been vouched for by some of the bar's patrons. You didn't have to cover for me."

Steven shrugged. "I simply said the first thing that came to mind."

Jessica rested her hand on the door knob. "I see. Are you sure you weren't establishing your own alibi for last night?"

Something resembling anger flashed in his eyes before disappearing as quickly as it arrived. "I'm sorry you feel that way."

Jessica suddenly felt like an ass. Steven had gone out of his way to help her at every turn, only to have her toss unwarranted accusations at him.

He moved to step around her, but Jess refused to budge. "I'm sorry, Steven. I didn't mean that."

"I think you did. It's obvious you don't trust me. Not that I blame you after learning about Melanie and me."

"You're wrong," she whispered softly, blocking his exit. "I do trust you. Like you said, that happened sixteen years ago. I have no right to judge you. If anyone has the right to be suspicious, it should be you."

Steven stopped in his attempt to leave. "I don't think you killed Eustice Martin anymore than I believe you had anything to do with Sandy Weaver's death. I don't know how I know, I just do."

Blowing out a shaky breath, Jessica tilted her head back enough to look into his eyes. "I really am sorry for what I said."

He slowly leaned down and brushed his lips across hers.

Jessica froze, unsure of what to do next. On one hand, she wanted to lean into him, to give someone else control of her tattered emotions for a while. But an image of Owen's handsome face stopped her.

She turned her head to the side, effectively ending the kiss. "I'll just go grab some of my things."

Chapter Thirty-Eight

Owen pulled into his drive after work that evening to find Jessica's car gone. Apparently, she'd come home at some point during the day and retrieved it.

Switching off the engine, he climbed out, sifted through his keys as he made his way to the porch, and let himself inside.

He could smell her essence in the house as he did every time he walked through the door.

A deep-seated pain sliced through him with the knowledge that he'd likely lost Jessica for good.

Owen didn't blame his wife for running out on him. Whether she was guilty of wrong doing or not, she had to feel betrayed after he'd Baker Acted her.

He told himself he'd done the right thing by having her mentally evaluated. But Owen wasn't so sure anymore.

The Jessica he'd loved since college, would never do the things he'd accused her of. But that didn't change the fact that she had admitted to seeing ghosts, broken into the neighbor's house, and traveled to another state to visit the very psychic whose body had later been found stabbed to death.

Owen stopped to stare at the wall above the sofa. According to the police, the message left there had been written in animal blood, though no animal had been recovered.

Could Jessica really do such a thing? Owen wondered, forcing his gaze away from the now clean wall.

He trailed off down the hall, coming to a stop in the doorway of their bedroom. The drawers hung open on Jessica's dresser, empty of their contents save for a red shirt neatly folded in the top one.

Owen's stomach tightened with sorrow. He moved deeper into the room until he stood in front of the dresser.

"Ah, Jess," he whispered, reaching into the drawer and wrapping his fingers around that red shirt. He brought it to his nose, took a deep breath and drew her lingering scent deep into his lungs.

Tears of anger and resentment sprang to his eyes. He had lost everything he'd ever cared about. First his precious son Jacob, and now his beautiful wife, Jessica.

Covering his face with the red shirt he'd bought her for her last birthday, Owen gave in to the overwhelming pain gripping his heart. His legs gave out beneath him and he slid to the floor in a cry of denial.

* * * *

Owen wasn't sure how long he sat on his
bedroom floor before he realized that darkness
had fully descended. Numb to his very soul, he
lacked the strength needed to push himself to
his feet.

Reaching into the pocket of his pants, he
pulled his cellphone free, slid his thumb across
the screen and selected Jessica's number. He
typed out a text. *Can we please talk? I'm sorry,
Jessica. God, I'm so sorry. I love you.*

The doorbell rang just then, startling
Owen out of his tormented thoughts.

Using the dresser for leverage, he pushed
himself to his feet and practically ran down the
hallway on numb, tingling legs.

"Jess?" he breathed, unlocking the door
and yanking it open.

Disappointment was swift as he took in
Marge's nosy expression. "Mrs. Hawthorn," he

greeted, unable to hide the despondency in his voice.

Marge stood on the porch wearing her usual green robe and hair rollers. "I came to see if you were alright."

Masking his emotions, Owen responded as calmly as he could manage under the circumstances. "I'm fine. Why would you ask?"

"Well, after your wife showed up here with that tall, good looking fellow and left with several suitcases, I assumed there was trouble in paradise."

Jealousy tore through Owen. He had no doubt the tall, good looking fellow Marge mentioned was the same man he'd seen in the elevator with Jessica.

He moved to close the door. "I appreciate your concern, Mrs. Hawthorn, but everything is fine. Now, if you'll excuse me."

"Didn't look fine to me," she sniffed, lifting her chin.

Owen hesitated. "What are you trying to say?"

She peered up at him, her face pinched in a disapproving manner. "From what I could see from my front yard, they kissed in this very doorway before they left earlier."

Owen's jealousy was soon replaced with a fury so deep he found it impossible to respond to Marge. He closed the door in her face.

A roar of denial ripped from his lungs. He drew back his arm and slammed his fist into the wall next to the door.

Pain exploded through his hand, but he didn't care. It paled in comparison to the agony his heart felt over Jessica's betrayal.

Cradling his now throbbing hand against his chest, Owen stumbled to the kitchen and took down a bottle of whiskey from the top of the refrigerator. He didn't bother with a glass, instead, he twisted off the cap and brought the bottle to his lips.

The alcohol burned all the way to his gut. Still, he continued to drink.

He staggered into the dining room and dropped heavily onto a chair. With images of his wife in another man's arms, Owen allowed his pain to consume him.

He turned up the bottle once again.

Chapter Thirty-Nine

Jessica stared at her three suitcases resting on the extra bed in her dumpy motel room. After what had happened in the doorway of her home earlier that morning, she couldn't bring herself to return to Steven's guesthouse.

He'd kissed her. Steven Ruckle had touched his mouth to hers before she realized his intent.

Though she'd enjoyed the sensation of being wanted, it wasn't her husband's lips touching hers. It had felt wrong...as if she'd betrayed Owen somehow.

Leaving the motel room, Jessica retrieved her paint supplies along with her easel and a couple of blank canvases from the back of her SUV and returned to the room.

She set up a place on the small table near the kitchenette and mixed up several different colors.

Plucking up a brush, she dipped it into the paint and touched it to the canvas. The first pattern of clouds began to form.

* * * *

The trill of a phone ringing penetrated Jessica's numb brain. She blinked to clear her vision, her eyes slowly focusing on the picture sitting before her.

She tilted her head to the side, taking in the image of a small gray cabin situated on the bank of a lake.

Why she'd painted the picture was beyond her. Jess had never been to nor seen the lakefront cabin before.

Something else caught her eye. She squinted at the still waters of the pond she'd created, and her breath caught. The reflection of a face stared back at her from the water's surface. Terry Dayton's face.

Jess pushed to her feet, her legs trembling beneath her. What did it all mean? she wondered in more than a little shock.

Then she noticed another reflection, not far from Terry's. Though the face wasn't clear enough to make out any details, she was fairly certain it belonged to a young girl.

She glanced at the clock, realizing it was after midnight. She couldn't possibly call Steven at that time of night. He would surely be sleeping.

Jessica sat back down in front of her latest creation, her gaze sweeping over every inch of that canvas. What was she supposed to do now? She could call the police, but tell them what? *I unknowingly painted a picture of a cabin with two people's reflections in the water? One of them, I'm fairly sure, is Terry Dayton's.* They would have her hauled back to the Sparkleberry Hills Mental Institution faster than she could blink.

She could take the painting to Melanie. But there again, she ran the risk of Melanie turning her in as well.

No, Jess needed to speak to Jasper. She'd seen the curiosity in his eyes, had no doubt that he'd wanted to hear what she had to say. But how to get him alone and away from his wife?

With a sigh of exhaustion, Jess stood once more and ambled over to the bed free of suitcases.

She peeled out of her clothes, pulled back the covers, and climbed onto the less than comfortable mattress. Her eyes slid shut and darkness claimed her before she could turn off the bedside lamp.

* * * *

Jessica awoke the following morning with a pounding headache and gritty eyes that felt like they'd been scrubbed with sandpaper.

She rolled over and glanced at the small alarm clock that sat on the nightstand between the two beds. It was two in the afternoon. She'd slept half the day away.

Throwing back the covers, she stood and padded across the room in her bra and panties to find the painting wasn't merely some dream she'd had in the middle of the night. It was definitely real, and just exactly as she remembered it.

Touching the now dry canvas, she gently ran her fingertip across the boy's reflection in the water and then touched on the female's face as well.

The longer she stared at the images before her, the harder her heart began to pound.

"What is happening to me?" she whispered in confusion, staggering back a few steps.

Jessica spun around and unzipped one of her suitcases with unsteady hands. She grabbed up a clean change of clothes, made her way to the bathroom, and showered.

Once clean, Jessica dressed in jeans, a white silk blouse with matching flats and then pulled her hair back into a ponytail. She bypassed her makeup, opting to wear sunglasses instead.

Snatching up the latest painting, Jessica loaded it into the backseat of her SUV next to the previous image she'd painted of Terry Dayton in that shallow grave.

She opened the driver's door, tossed her purse onto the passenger seat, and got behind the wheel.

Steven picked that moment to turn into the parking lot of the motel. He pulled up next to her and rolled down his window.

Jessica lowered hers as well. "What are you doing here?"

"I tried calling you last night, but you didn't answer. Nor did you answer this morning. I figured you were still upset with me about what happened yesterday."

She knew exactly what he referred to. "I'm assuming you mean the almost kiss."

Disappointment flickered in his eyes. "Yeah."

"I'm not upset with you, Steven. I just have a lot on my mind…a lot to think through."

Steven's elbow came up to rest along his door frame. "And I'm a complication you don't need right now."

"I didn't say that. Look, Steven, you've been a Godsend through all this, and as attractive as I find you, it doesn't change the fact that I'm a married woman."

He glanced down at the ground for a moment before returning his disappointed gaze to hers. "In case you've forgotten, your husband had you locked up in the mental ward against your will."

Jessica inwardly flinched. She didn't need to be reminded of Owen's damnable Baker Acting of her person. "I haven't forgotten, and I'm not sure I'll ever forgive him for what he did, but in his defense, he thought he was doing what was best for me."

"How can you defend him after what he did?"

"I'm not defending him, Steven. I'm only saying that had I been in his position, I might have done the same thing. Especially if I thought it would keep him alive. Owen has experienced the unthinkable where I'm concerned." She couldn't bring herself to mention the attempted suicide she'd put Owen through only two years before.

Steven opened his car door and got out. He leaned in the window of her SUV and cupped the side of her face. "I didn't mean to sound insensitive. I just want you to know that I'm here for you if you need me." He paused. "For anything."

Jessica stared back at him from behind the safety of her sunglasses. He was everything any woman could ask for. Handsome, successful, and charismatic. But he wasn't Owen. "Thank you, Steven. That means a lot."

He straightened away from the door. "Where are you headed?"

She wondered how much to tell him. The last thing she wanted was him following her to the Daytons' house and causing trouble. Yet the longer she sat there gazing up at him, the more she wanted to tell him. "I'm going to see Jasper."

Steven's eyebrows lifted. "What for?"

Jessica jerked her thumb toward the backseat. "To show him my latest painting."

Steven opened the back door to her SUV, retrieved the painting and studied it for several heartbeats. "Why would you want him to see this?"

Jessica climbed out and joined Steven in his perusal of the painting he held. "I painted it late last night. See the faces in the water?"

Lifting the canvas higher, Steven squinted at the image. "I see them. What does it mean?"

"I have no idea, but it has something to do with Terry Dayton's disappearance."

Appearing unconvinced, Steven set the painting back onto the seat and shut the door. "Are you sure you didn't subconsciously dream this one up? I'm not saying it doesn't have something to do with Terry Dayton, but the last image you created, Terry was in a shallow grave, not a lake."

Doubt quickly trickled in. "Maybe so, but this is the second time I've painted something with no recollection of it during or after. And both times had to do with Terry Dayton..." Her voice trailed off.

"Jessica," Steven began, only to falter. He tried again. "Look, maybe you should try to put Terry's disappearance behind you for a little while. At least until we can clear up the suspicion surrounding Sandy Weaver's murder."

Climbing back behind the wheel of her SUV, Jessica closed her door. "I'll give it some thought."

"That's all I ask. Will you stop by later tonight and have dinner with me?"

Jessica nodded and put the SUV in gear. "I'll text you when I'm headed your way."

"Be careful."

Chapter Forty

Jessica nibbled at the food she'd picked up in the drive-thru and drove around for over an hour, periodically driving past the Dayton home in hopes that she'd catch Jasper's truck in the driveway.

Her mind continued to drift back to her conversation with Steven in the parking lot of her motel.

He'd seemed out of sorts, antsy and almost...nervous. He had grown even more unsettled after seeing the latest of Jessica's paintings.

A strange feeling swept over her in that moment. Why the sudden change in his demeanor? There had been a certain desperation in his eyes, as if he hadn't wanted her to speak with Jasper.

She supposed what she sensed in Steven could have been jealousy or resentment over the fact that she'd planned on visiting the Dayton's without first consulting with him about it.

Shaking off her unsettling thoughts, Jessica made another sweep around the Daytons' neighborhood when she noticed Melanie standing out front, her arms crossed over her chest.

Jessica cringed, realizing she'd been caught stalking them.

With no choice but to stop or play ignorant and drive on past, Jess pulled up along the curb and got out.

Melanie unfolded her arms as Jessica approached. "How many trips were you planning on making before you stopped?"

Embarrassed to the roots of her hair, Jessica muttered, "As many as it would take until Jasper arrived home."

"I see." Melanie's gaze swept over Jessica's attire. "Any particular reason why you wish to speak to my husband and not me?"

Left with little choice but to be honest, that's exactly what Jessica did. "I knew you would become angry. I also knew you wouldn't believe what I had to say."

Uncertainty flashed in Melanie's eyes before they blanked of expression. "You're probably right, but you might as well spill it."

Unsure of what to say next, Jessica held up a finger. "I just need to grab some things from my car."

"Fine. Go ahead."

Jessica jogged across the Daytons' yard, terrified and filled with anxiety. She had no doubt that when Melanie saw the two paintings Jess had in her SUV, she would lose her temper, and most likely call the authorities. *Damn.*

The sound of a vehicle pulling into the drive caught Jessica's attention. She snagged the two paintings in the backseat and turned to find Jasper emerging from his truck.

Relief was instant.

Jasper waved as he trekked across the lawn to stand next to his wife.

Jess returned the greeting, closed the door to her SUV, and hurried back to Melanie's side.

"What's going on?" Jasper placed his arm around his wife's shoulder.

Melanie spoke before Jessica had a chance to respond. "Mrs. Nobles has something she wants to speak with us about."

Jasper sent Jessica a reassuring smile. "Come on in. No sense in us standing around in the yard. It's about to rain."

Jess hadn't noticed the clouds gathering in the darkened skies, but she did then.

Thunder picked that moment to roll in, followed by a flash of lightning.

Jasper spun toward the front door. "We'd better hurry."

Jessica followed the Daytons into the oversized living room. Too nervous to sit, she opted to stand next to a dark brown recliner.

Melanie and Jasper took a seat next to each other on the couch.

"What do you have there?" Jasper nodded to the paintings Jessica held in her hands.

Clearing her throat, Jessica met Melanie's gaze. "The first time we met, I told you of how I saw your son in the window of the house next door to me."

Melanie's expression became closed off. Though, she didn't speak, she continued to watch Jessica as if waiting on her to get to the point.

That's exactly what Jessica did. "The night I saw him in that upstairs window, I went into my office intending to paint a portrait of my son, Jacob. I blacked out at some point, and when I came to, I was still holding the paint brush in my hand. But instead of Jacob's image on the canvas, I'd somehow painted this..." She turned the painting toward Jasper and Melanie.

Melanie cried out, her hand slapping over her mouth. Tears welled up in her eyes and her body began to tremble. She shook her head, lowering her hand from her mouth. "What kind of sick game is this?"

Jessica couldn't speak around the lump welling up in her throat. She set the painting on the floor to rest against her leg and then reached out a hand toward Melanie Dayton.

Springing to her feet, Melanie fled the room in a flurry of tears and heart wrenching sobs.

"I'm so sorry," Jessica wheezed, barely able to get the words out.

Jasper, though pale and obviously shaken, remained on the couch. He lifted his gaze to Jessica. "You painted Terry's grave?"

When Jessica simply stood there, staring back at him through her tears, he nodded toward her other hand. "And that one? What is that?"

"This was a bad idea," Jess choked out. "I'll just be going now."

Jasper unsteadily got to his feet, rounded the coffee table and stopped in front of Jess. "Show me."

Jessica shook her head. "I made a mistake. Please—"

"Show me!"

Taking a step back, Jessica lifted the painting she still held and turned it to face Jasper Dayton.

He peered down at the image for so long, Jessica was beginning to think he'd become hypnotized by it.

Jasper lifted his gaze to Jessica's. "What is this?"

Jess wasn't sure if she should be relieved that Jasper didn't recognize the place she'd painted, or worried that Steven had been right, and she'd subconsciously created the image from a dream she'd had. "It doesn't look familiar to you?"

"Should it?" Jasper rumbled, obviously confused.

Jessica lowered the picture. "I suppose not. I'm sorry I bothered you."

Lightning popped somewhere nearby, sending nerves scattering through Jessica's body. She glanced toward the window, noticing how dark it had grown in the short time she'd been there.

Jasper's gaze flicked to the window as well. "I'm going to check on Melanie. You'd better get going if you hope to get ahead of this storm."

"I'm really sorry I upset your wife, Mr. Dayton. Truly, that wasn't my intention. I won't bother either of you again. You can rest assured." She picked up the painting propped against her leg and turned to go.

"Melanie is a good person, Mrs. Nobles. She just can't accept that Terry isn't coming back."

Jessica reached for the doorknob, peering at him over her shoulder. "Have you?"

"Accepted that he's not coming back?"

"Yes," she softly responded.

"A long time ago." With that, he moved off in the direction his wife had disappeared.

Jessica opened the door and stepped onto the front porch of the pale-yellow home before making a run for her vehicle.

She set the two paintings in the backseat and hurried around to the driver's side door.

Lightning popped again, scaring the daylights out of her. She quickly climbed in, slid behind the wheel, breathing a sigh of relief as she made it inside the SUV just seconds ahead of the pouring rain.

Jessica started the engine and turned on the windshield wipers, her gaze landing on her cell phone resting on the console.

Snatching it up, she swiped her thumb across the screen. Her heart stuttered as Owen's digits appeared.

She wanted nothing more than to hear his voice, to tell him how sorry she was for not being honest with him. But she couldn't bring herself to do it.

Jessica had been a needy baggage of instability for the past three and a half years. No matter how insane she'd felt or how hopeless things had become, Owen had been by her side through it all. But Jess had broken him. She'd seen it in his eyes...heard it in his voice.

Owen deserved better. He deserved someone stable, someone capable of intimacy and passion. Not some mentally unstable individual who saw spirits and painted images of the dead.

Dropping her forehead against the steering wheel, Jessica allowed her tears to flow. She cried for Jacob, for little Terry Dayton and his parents. But most of all, she cried for Owen. Jasper Dayton may have lost his only son, but he still had his wife. Poor Owen had no one.

He'd lost everything that had ever mattered to him.

"I love you, Owen. I'm so sorry…"

Jessica wasn't sure how long she sat there, crying in the rain before she gathered her resolve and lifted her head.

She pulled the gearshift down to drive and eased away from the curb. She would go back to the motel, gather her things and head back to Chicago where she couldn't hurt Owen any longer.

With her mind made up, Jessica switched on the defrost, squinted through the rain at the oncoming headlights and took a left at the stop sign.

Chapter Forty-One

Owen paced along the foot of his bed, a bottle of whiskey dangling from his hand.

He caught a glimpse of his reflection in the mirror on his next pass across the carpeted floor. He looked like hell.

Turning up the bottle, Owen reveled in the burn of the whiskey as it slid down his throat. It told him two things. He was still alive, and he'd be in a comfortable state of numbness in the next thirty minutes.

His gaze touched on a photo of Jessica, perched on his nightstand in the pale wooden frame he'd carved for her some years back.

He rounded the bed and plucked up the photo. "Ah, Jess. My beautiful Jessica."

Tears of sorrow gathered in his eyes. He'd lost his wife just as he lost his son. She might not be gone in the same sense as Jacob, but she'd left him nonetheless.

He dropped his weight onto the mattress, hugging the image close to his chest and took another long pull of the blessed whiskey.

Thunder boomed in the distance, drawing his attention to the window. The Dayton house sat in his line of sight, silhouetted by the flash of lightning streaking across the sky.

Owen laid the picture he held on the bed next to him and stood. He moved closer to the window, unable to take his gaze from the desolate looking house that stood before him.

Jessica had become obsessed with that place—obsessed to the point she'd broken into it to reach a boy that had been missing for over a decade.

Lightning flashed again, illuminating the upstairs windows. But nothing appeared save for the rain washing down its panes.

Pushing away from the sight, Owen meandered off down the hall to stop at the door to the office. He flipped on the light and moved into the room.

Setting the bottle of whiskey down on the corner of the desk, Owen opened the lid to Jessica's laptop.

It booted up to the sign on screen, prompting him for a passcode. He typed in *JACOB,* knowing without a doubt that Jessica would choose their son's name as her password.

The computer quickly loaded to the last page Jessica had visited. *Seven-year-old Terry Dayton went missing on January tenth...*

Owen continued to read, somehow feeling closer to Jess with every word he consumed.

A thought occurred to him the longer he sat there reading about the missing Dayton boy. He immediately visited the computer's history.

Every page that Jessica had loaded could be found there, including one that read *STEVEN RUCKLE.*

Owen clicked on the name, stunned to find the face of the man he'd seen in the elevator with Jess.

Anger and jealousy warred inside him the longer he studied the image of the man before him. Anger won out.

He snatched up a piece of paper, along with a pen and jotted down Steven's name.

Clicking out of that screen, Owen did a reverse name lookup on the computer and pulled up Steven's address. He entered it into his phone's GPS.

With phone in hand, he jumped to his feet, closed the laptop lid, and rushed from the office to grab his keys from a hook in the kitchen.

Owen opened the side door in the living room and pressed the button on the wall in the garage. The garage door instantly began to rise, revealing the pelting rain now flooding his drive.

He rounded the front of his car, hopped inside, and inserted the key into the ignition. The engine revved to life with the flick of his wrist.

Owen eased out of the garage, switching on the windshield wipers as he backed down his driveway and entered the street beyond. He would pay Mr. Ruckle a visit. If the ex-reporter thought to take Owen's wife from him, he'd better be prepared to fight, because Owen wasn't giving up on a Jess without one.

The rain picked up to the point Owen had to slow his speed or end up in a ditch somewhere. He could barely see two feet in front of the car. Still, he pressed on. He wasn't returning home without Jessica, no matter what he had to drive through to reach her.

Holding his cellphone in a death grip, Owen followed the prompts from the GPS and took a left at the next intersection. Five minutes later, he pulled into a circle drive of a two-story brick home.

The house appeared dark and no vehicles were present that Owen could see.

He snarled a few curse words and laid on the horn. Nothing moved inside the house.

More than a little furious, he slammed the palm of his hand against the steering wheel, his mind spinning with unimaginable scenarios. *Where could they be?*

Owen swiped his finger across the screen of his cellphone and selected Jessica's number. Of course, it went straight to voicemail.

Pressing the end key, he pulled up her number once more and sent her a text. *Jess, please call me. I love you.*

He lowered the phone to the console, unsure of where to go next.

Maybe she's at a motel, he thought, snatching up the phone once more. He touched the icon for their personal banking and waited for it to load. After entering the expected information, he scrolled through the charges until he found what he sought. *Country Inn Motor Lodge.*

With determination and more than a little fear of what he'd find, Owen sped out of Ruckle's drive and shot down the street in the midst of the torrential downpour. Jessica was coming home with him if he had to drag her kicking and screaming. If she wanted him to beg, he would beg. He would do whatever it took to get her back, even if that meant he had to take out Ruckle to make that happen.

Chapter Forty-Two

Jessica's cellphone vibrated, telling her that she had a text message. Without taking her gaze from what little of the road she could see, she felt around on the seat until she gripped her phone in her hand.

Swiping her finger across the screen, she opened the text to find a message from Owen. *Jess, please call me. I love you.*

Relief swept through her. Owen still loved her, no matter what she'd done or how crazy she had acted.

She pressed reply and lifted her thumb to the phone's digital keyboard.

Bright lights suddenly shot up behind her, momentarily blinding her.

Jessica dropped her phone, gripping the wheel with both hands as the lights grew rapidly closer.

An ear-piercing sound vibrated through the car as the fast-approaching vehicle slammed into the back of her.

The airbag exploded in her face, sending excruciating pain shooting through her skull.

She had a split second to silently cry out before the car went airborne and her world turned black.

* * * *

Jessica moaned in pain as her body was jostled around on a hard surface. She attempted to open her eyes, but something held them closed. It took her a moment to realize they were swollen shut.

She strained to recall what had happened. Memory of leaving the Daytons and driving in the rain was all Jess could grab onto.

But then bits and pieces of random images sparked behind her closed eyelids. Melanie's reaction to the painting, the crack of lightning as she got into her car. The text from Owen. The rapidly approaching headlights in her rearview mirror. Someone had run into her car at a high rate of speed. *Oh, my God.*

Jessica tried opening her mouth to cry out for help, but her lips wouldn't move. Nor would her hands and feet she realized in terror. She'd been bound and gagged.

Panic quickly set in, sending her mind into a place it wasn't prepared to go. She struggled against her bonds to no avail while trying to breathe through the blood trickling from her nose.

Her lungs hurt along with her head.

I have to calm down. Think, Jessica, you have to think.

It took considerable effort to pull herself together enough to keep from blacking out. Her lungs felt as if they would explode from lack of precious oxygen, and her mind continued to rebel against what she knew to be true. Someone had tried to kill her.

It suddenly dawned on her that she was in the trunk of a moving car. It bounced along an uneven surface, telling her one thing for certain...they were definitely not on the highway.

Jessica could do nothing but lie there bound and gagged while waiting for the vehicle to stop. Yet she knew exactly what would happen then...she would be killed just as Sandy Weaver had.

Tears welled up behind Jessica's closed eyes to leak from the swollen corners. She would never again have the chance to tell Owen how sorry she was for shutting him out, to let him know how much she loved him and always had.

The car finally rolled to an abrupt stop, sending pain shooting through Jessica's shoulders. She had no idea how long she'd been bound, but her arms had been screaming in agony since she'd became conscious.

Thunder boomed overhead, temporarily drowning out the sound of Jessica's thundering heart.

The engine shut off on the vehicle and the slam of a door followed shortly after.

A moan of fear vibrated behind Jessica's gag with the knowledge that she would soon face her abductor. The fact that she couldn't see kicked her anxiety up another notch.

The trunk abruptly opened, and the sting of the pelting rain hit Jessica in the face.

She was suddenly yanked up by her tormented arms. Jessica cried out from behind her gag as her stomach made contact with the unforgiving ball of a man's shoulder.

Nausea rolled with every step her captor took. She prayed to God she didn't vomit behind that gag and choke to death on it.

The man trudged through the rain for what seemed an eternity to an upside-down Jess before he entered some kind of shelter and dropped her trussed up weight on the floor at his feet.

Excruciating pain burst through Jessica's body, eliciting another cry from behind her gag.

The sound of footsteps could be heard moving away from her just seconds ahead of a door opening in the distance. It slammed closed, telling Jessica she'd been left alone on that floor. For how long, she had no idea.

Owen…

Chapter Forty-Three

Owen sat in the pouring rain in the parking lot of the *Country Inn Motor Lodge* staring at the door to room 102. He wasn't sure how long he'd sat there, waiting for Jessica to return before he decided to leave.

Cranking up his car, he reached for the gearshift when a dark colored sedan pulled into the parking space next to him.

Steven Ruckle jumped out, shielding his eyes from the rain and hurried up to the overhang of the motel.

Rage boiled inside Owen's blood. He opened his door and flew from the car before Ruckle realized what had happened.

Owen gripped the other man by the arm, jerked him around and slammed his fist against his face.

Steven staggered back a few feet before catching his footing. He lifted his hand to the corner of his mouth. "You son of a bitch," he growled, launching at Owen.

But Owen was a force to be reckoned with. He had too much to lose to allow Ruckle to take him down. He ducked, coming up with an uppercut that caught Steven on the chin.

"Where is she?" Owen snarled, spinning around behind the reporter.

Steven quickly faced him, his hands coming up to ward off the next potential punch. "I have no idea. That's why I'm here, looking for her."

Owen took a threatening step closer. "Bullshit. You know which motel room belongs to her, but you haven't seen her?"

"I saw her earlier this evening, but as per usual, she's not answering her calls or texts. So, I figured I'd see if she was here."

The longer Owen stood there looking into Ruckle's eyes, the angrier he became. "I won't give her up for you or anyone else. Do you understand? I'll kill you before I let you have her."

Something flickered in Ruckle's eyes. He lowered his hands and blew out a resigned breath. "Yeah, well you don't have to worry about killing me anytime soon. She made it perfectly clear that she didn't want me. Not for a lack of trying on my part, mind you."

Owen studied Ruckle's face closely but saw no hint of deception. He relaxed his stance. Somewhat. "Then what are you doing here?"

"I came to see how her visit with the Daytons went since she didn't answer her phone."

"Why did she go see the Daytons?"

Steven ran a hand through his wet hair. "She'd painted another picture the night before of a cabin on a lake. An eerie looking painting with the images of Terry Dayton's and some young girl's faces just beneath the surface of the water. It really shook her up. She wanted to speak with Jasper Dayton to see if he recognized the cabin in the painting."

Owen thought about that for a moment. *Surely to God Jessica didn't take her paranoia to the Daytons?* "Where do the Daytons live?"

Steven stepped around him and headed toward his car. "Come on. I'll show you."

With little choice but to do as the asshole said or sit in the rain and hope Jessica returned soon, Owen got back inside his car and followed Ruckle from the parking lot.

So Jess had turned Ruckle down, Owen mused, staying close behind the dark colored sedan. Did that mean she'd be willing to give

Owen another chance, or was she simply not interested in Ruckle? Owen wasn't sure about anything anymore. He did, however, know that he would do everything in his power to make Jessica happy again. Even if that meant moving her back to Chicago. He had yet to sell their home. He would even unpack Jacob's things, if that's what Jessica wanted. Owen only wanted her love.

Flashing lights could be seen up ahead through the torrential downpour. Owen touched on his breaks, staying close behind Ruckle as he eased along the side of the road, giving a wide berth to the fire trucks and police cars.

Owen squinted against the red and blue lights, wondering what had happened, but the downpouring of rain made it impossible to see.

* * * *

Owen slowed to a stop behind Ruckle's sedan as he parked in front of a pale-yellow house in a nice suburban neighborhood. The flash of lightning revealed a white work truck sitting in the drive, but Jessica's SUV was nowhere in sight.

Waiting for Ruckle to exit his vehicle, Owen quickly joined him. They ran across the yard toward the front porch, their shoes sloshing through the water puddling on the lawn.

Owen stepped onto the porch next to Ruckle and wiped the rain from his face while the other man rang the doorbell.

Long moments ticked by before the door opened to reveal a confused looking blonde. She blinked up at Ruckle, her eyes glassy and slightly unfocused. "Steven?"

It wasn't lost on Owen that woman knew Ruckle personally.

Steven responded in a smooth voice. "Hi, Melanie."

"What are you doing here?" Her words could barely be heard over the thunder rolling through the skies.

Ruckle stepped aside, tilting his head in Owen's direction. "This is Owen Nobles, Jessica's husband."

Melanie's gaze flicked to Owen. "What do you want?"

Owen cleared his throat, noticing the slight slur in the woman's voice. "I'm looking for my wife. I was told she came by here earlier."

"She showed up here waving a painting around and talking a bunch of nonsense."

Ruckle reached up and touched Melanie on the arm. "I know you're upset, but trust me when I say that hurting you was the last thing Jessica wanted to do."

Melanie shifted her attention back to Ruckle, and her eyes narrowed. "You knew she was coming here with that garbage?"

"I did. But she would never intentionally upset you, Melanie. She'd hoped to speak with Jasper to see if he would recognize the painting she'd done last night."

Melanie paled and staggered back a step. "That's just sick. Why would she want to show Jasper a painting of our son lying in a shallow grave?"

Steven glanced at Owen and then back to Melanie. "No...the other one. The one with the little gray cabin on the lake."

"A gray cabin on the lake," Melanie repeated in a wooden voice. She turned to look over her shoulder and stumbled slightly. "Jasper!"

Owen took a step forward. "Did Jessica say where she was going when she left here?"

Melanie called out to her husband once more, her gait unsteady. "Jasper!"

"Please," Owen interjected, drawing Melanie's attention back to him. "Anything you can remember will help. Did she say—"

"Jasper's not here." Melanie's dazed eyes grew more confused if that were possible.

More than a little frustrated, Owen ground out between clenched teeth. "Mrs. Dayton, did my wife give any indication where she might be heading when she left here?"

Melanie shook her head, her hand coming up to massage her left temple. She settled her unfocused gaze on Ruckle as if Owen hadn't spoken. "Why would she want to know about our cabin?"

Ruckle stilled. "Your cabin?"

"It's more Jasper's than mine. He spent a lot of time there before Terry disappeared…"

"Where is Jasper, now?" Ruckle demanded, suddenly gripping her upper arms.

Melanie squeezed her eyes tightly shut. "I don't know. I thought he was here."

"The cabin. Tell me how to get to the cabin."

Her eyelids lifted and Owen could see the tears forming there. She took a shuddering breath and then rattled off an address. "What's going on, Steven?"

Ruckle released her, spun on his heel, and sailed off the porch without answering.

"What are you not telling me?" Owen barked, catching up to Ruckle in a few short strides.

"I believe Jasper Dayton has Jessica!"

The bottom dropped out of Owen's stomach. "We'll take my car!"

Owen was behind the wheel and squealing tires before Steven's door finished closing.

"Talk to me," Owen demanded, switching on the defrost to clear the windshield.

Steven engaged his seatbelt. "Take a left at the four-way up ahead."

"Why the hell would Jasper have Jessica?" Owen snarled, turning at the four-way without slowing.

Ruckle gripped the dash with both hands. "The picture Jessica painted last night of the cabin on the lake? She took that painting to the Daytons this evening."

Owen listened as Ruckle explained everything that had happened recently, including the details of Jessica's recent painting.

Ruckle met his gaze. "That cabin belongs to Jasper Dayton."

"Son of a bitch," Owen growled, his mind conjuring up everything Jess had told him over the past few weeks. "She tried to tell me, but I wouldn't hear her. I had her locked in a mental ward, for God's sake." He floored the gas pedal.

Ruckle continued to grip that dash. "Don't let your guilt get us killed, man. Pay attention to the damn road."

But Owen was no longer listening. His mind could think of nothing but Jessica and how he'd unintentionally pushed her away. If something happened to her because of his idiocy, Owen would never forgive himself. He drove faster. "Call the police."

"And tell them what? We have no proof of anything. All we have are two paintings from a woman who's a suspect in a murder case. Not to mention she just spent three days in the mental hospital. Trust me, they won't come rushing out here with guns drawn."

Owen felt sick. "Call them anyway!"

Ruckle dug his cellphone from the pocket of his pants and dialed 911.

Owen listened as he gave them the address to the cabin.

"I don't know," Ruckle growled into the phone after giving the dispatcher what information he knew. "Just hurry." He ended the call.

"How much farther is this damn cabin?" Owen felt as if they'd been driving for hours.

"Approximately five more minutes. Turn right just beyond those railroad tracks up ahead."

A flash of lightning revealed a wash out in the road. Owen slammed on breaks a second too late. He lost control of the car, fighting to hold onto the wheel as they spun violently off the side of the road.

With his breath punching in and out of his chest, Owen pressed the gas, only to realize the tires were spinning in the mud.

A string of curses soon filled the car. "Son of a bitch, we're stuck!"

Jerking open the door, Owen jumped out. "Hurry," he snarled, already breaking into a run.

Chapter Forty-Four

Jessica rolled to her side in an attempt to relieve some of the pain in her shoulders. She wasn't sure how long she'd been bound and gagged, but her arms had gone to sleep long ago, sending sharp prickly pains shooting through her hands.

She gritted her teeth, straining to open her eyes enough to check out her surroundings.

The door abruptly opened, and the sound of footballs echoed inside the room. "You're awake."

Jessica's heart stuttered in stunned disbelief. She angled her head in the direction of Jasper Dayton's voice. She wanted to cry out, to beg him to release her, but the gag in her mouth held her back.

The thumping of his boots grew closer, terrifying Jess and drawing a whimper from her throat. She blinked through her swollen lids, barely able to discern his features in the dim light surrounding him.

He dropped to his haunches next to her and removed the gag from her mouth. "I'm sure you're wondering why you're here."

Jessica swallowed around her confusion and terror. "My arms," she gasped in torment. "Please…"

His sigh blew the hair back from her face. She could smell his cologne as he leaned over her and severed the bonds at her wrists.

Jessica cried out with the burn of the sudden feeling that shot up her arms. She rolled to her back, her teeth locked together in agony.

"It didn't have to be this way, Jessica. If you'd simply stopped nosing around where you didn't belong, none of this would be happening now."

Finding her voice, Jessica croaked, "I don't understand. Why are you doing this?"

Instead of answering right away, Jasper took hold of the hem of her shirt and wiped the blood away from her nose. "I'm pretty sure that airbag broke your nose."

An image of headlights rushing up behind her—the car slamming into the back of her SUV, lit through her mind. "You ran me off the road." It wasn't a question.

"You left me no choice. This is all your fault, Jessica. Sandy Weaver, Eustice Martin, all of it."

Jessica squinted up at him. "What are you talking about?" Her gaze flicked to the knife Jasper held in his hand.

He glanced down at the blade and without warning, cut the bonds at Jessica's feet. "Get up."

"J-Jasper…"

Gripping her by the hair, Jasper yanked her upright and then shoved her toward the door. "Move."

Jessica stumbled to her knees, so great was her terror. It took her several tries to push back to her feet. "What's happening, Jasper? I—"

The click of a hammer being cocked shut down the rest of Jessica's plea.

She staggered forward in fear and disbelief, opened the door and stepped out into the rain.

"Keep moving," Jasper demanded, pressing his weapon between her shoulder blades.

Jessica trudged through the mud, her gaze on the moonlight reflecting off the water's surface up ahead. "What are you going to do with me?"

"What I should have done in the beginning."

Jessica opened her mouth to keep him talking when her gaze landed on a shovel resting next to a deep hole in the earth a few feet ahead of her.

She dug in her heels, spinning around to face him. "Oh, my God. Please, Jasper. I don't know why you're doing this, but I'll do anything. Just tell me what you want from me."

"Get in the hole, Jessica."

A sob escaped her. Tears of terror spilled from her eyes to mingle with the rain tracking down her face. She glanced at the pistol he held and then shifted her gaze back to his face. "I'm begging you, Jasper!"

He took a step closer, raising the gun higher. "Get in the fucking hole."

An image of a smiling Owen flashed through Jessica's mind—a smile she would never have a chance to look upon again. She stepped into the hole.

"I really don't enjoy having to do this," Jasper admitted in an offhanded manner.

Jessica took a shuddering breath, scared beyond anything she'd ever experienced before. "Then don't. Please. I won't tell anyone."

"It's far too late for that. Someone has to take the blame for Sandy and Eustice Martin's deaths."

Understanding dawned. "You killed Sandy and Eustice? But why?"

"When Melanie told me about your unexpected visit to see her, and that you'd tracked down Sandy Weaver, I had to do something to stop you from digging deeper. So I killed Sandy, knowing full well the police would find your fingerprints there."

He continued speaking, his finger caressing the trigger of his gun. "Eustice was simply a casualty of circumstance. Once the police find the knife that killed him and Sandy, they'll spend the next decade searching for you."

Jessica thought about poor Owen, and how he would spend the rest of his life thinking his wife murdered two people. "Why kill those people just to frame me? It makes no sense. All I ever wanted was to find out what happened to your son."

Jasper rolled his head on his neck as if Jessica's words struck a cord in him. "You really want to know what happened to my son? I had him killed."

The ground tilted beneath Jessica's feet. She covered her mouth with her hand to hold back the cry that rose in her throat.

"I had no choice," Jasper murmured, rubbing at his forehead with his free hand. "He'd seen something he shouldn't. I couldn't risk him telling his mother. I would have spent the rest of my life in prison if I didn't die in the electric chair first."

His manic gaze locked on Jessica once more. "I'm a monster, Mrs. Nobles. As was Eustice. For years, we traveled to different states, abducting young girls and selling them to the highest bidder."

"Sex trafficking," Jessica whispered through numb lips.

Jasper shrugged. "Something like that. We made a lot of money in those few short years. Until Eustice started damaging the merchandise...which significantly lowered their value on the market if they survived at all."

Bile rushed into Jessica's mouth. She leaned forward and heaved into her waiting grave.

"The last girl we brought home," Jasper continued as if discussing the weather, "was a pretty one. I decided to keep her in my basement overnight to ensure Eustice didn't damage or kill her. I never dreamed that Terry would wake up and find her down there."

More horror slammed into Jessica. Terry had witnessed the little girl's terror at the hands of his own father.

Jasper took a step forward, his weapon aimed at Jessica's chest. "You see? He left me no choice. He began crying, growing hysterical. I was afraid he would wake Melanie. So, I took him to Eustice to take care of."

"You had Eustice kill your only child?" Jessica cried, unable to keep the horror from her voice. "What did he do to him?"

Jasper nodded to a place on Jessica's left. "He's buried there next to that willow tree."

"The little girl," Jess choked out. "The girl who's face I saw in the lake?"

"There's more than one girl in that lake." He pulled the trigger.

An explosion rocked Jessica's skull, and something slammed into her body with a force that took her feet out from under her.

She couldn't inhale, couldn't move or think. Her eyes began to roll back in her head until she knew nothing more.

Chapter Forty-Five

The sound of gunfire ricocheted through the trees, followed by the rumble of distant thunder.

"Jessica!" Owen shouted, vaulting over a downed fence now illuminated by the lightning.

He could hear Ruckle running through the brush behind him, his labored breathing, mirroring Owen's own.

Owen suddenly burst through a clearing, his legs eating up the ground as he raced toward a small cabin in the distance.

"I'll check around back," Ruckle barked, sailing past the open door of the cabin.

Owen burst inside, his gaze scanning the interior of the place to find it empty.

He rushed back into the rain and ran toward the lake he'd seen in the distance.

Another shot rang out, sending Owen's heart into his throat. "Jessicaaaa!"

More lightning arced across the sky, illuminating a figure holding a gun.

"That's far enough," the figure snarled from the shadows.

Owen skidded to a stop, nearly falling over Ruckle, who lay still at his feet. "Where's my wife?"

"You must be Owen. Jessica's dead, same as Steven." He nodded toward Ruckle's downed form.

A moan of denial ripped from Owen's chest. He jumped over Ruckle's body, not caring that he would die next. "Fuck you, you piece of shit!"

A deafening explosion resonated through Owen's head, followed by another and yet another. With every shot that rang out, Jasper's body violently jerked until he dropped limply to his back.

Owen spun in a half circle, his gaze scanning the darkness beyond. There was someone else out there, someone besides Jasper. It took him a moment to realize his legs shook too much for him to stand. He dropped to his knees in the mud.

Melanie staggered from the shadows still holding a gun in her trembling hands.

"He killed my baby," she groaned, emptying two more rounds into Jasper's body. "He killed my Terry..." She began to sob uncontrollably before crumpling to heap next to Jasper.

Owen crawled forward on his hands and knees, searching the darkness for signs of Jessica. She couldn't be dead, he mentally chanted...she just couldn't be.

Another lightning strike provided enough light to see the hole in the earth ahead.

Owen scrambled closer until his upper body hung over the edge. He could see the outline of a body huddled inside.

In a panic, he threw his legs over the side, careful not to step on Jessica. And he knew it to be Jess as surely as he knew he would die without her.

"Ah, God, Jess...no." Tucking an arm behind her head and one beneath her knees, he lifted her wet, muddied body high against his chest and climbed from that hole.

He didn't slow until he nearly ran into a white truck parked around back of the cabin. He opened the passenger side door, crying anew as the interior light spilled across Jessica's bloodied form.

"Jess?" he choked out, pressing his ear against her muddied lips. The slightest hint of breath could be felt tickling his skin.

She lived. His Jessica was still alive.

Owen gently laid her on the seat, quickly shut the door, and ran around to the driver's side. He jumped behind the wheel and pulled Jessica's head onto his lap.

Putting the truck in reverse, Owen gave it as much gas as he could without burying the tires in the mud, and then circled the cabin. "Hang on, baby. I'm gonna get you some help!"

The headlights of the truck touched on Melanie Dayton long enough for Owen to see her lift the gun to her head and pull the trigger. She dropped limply across Jasper's body.

But Owen had no time to dwell on the Daytons. Jessica was hurt, and he needed to get her some help before it was too late.

He pressed the accelerator and drove toward the main road with every prayer he could think of falling from his lips.

Flashing lights and sirens were a relief to Owen's terrified soul as he rounded a corner to find a convoy of police cars headed toward him. He pulled the truck to the edge of the gravel road while tears of relief leaked from his eyes. "They're here, Jess. Help is here."

Chapter Forty-Six

Jessica woke to a painful throbbing sensation in her shoulder. She moved to lift her arm, but the pain became unbearable.

"Easy," Owen soothed, his face appearing above her. "Try not to move."

She focused on Owen's eyes, her thoughts scattered and fuzzy. "Where am I?"

"You're in the hospital, Jess."

"Hospital?" she repeated, noticing a beeping sound near her head.

Owen gaze softened, and he bent to brush his lips across her forehead. "You're fine now. You're going to be alright."

Memory began to creep back in and the beeping noise next to her head picked up its pace. "He shot me. Jasper Dayton shot me."

"Nurse?" Owen called out, his voice filled with concern. He leaned in close to Jessica's face once more. "It's okay, Jess. He's gone. He can never hurt you again."

Images of Jasper holding that gun on her swirled through Jessica's head. She shuddered with the memory of falling into that mud-filled grave.

"Mrs. Nobles?" A nurse appeared in Jessica's line of vision. "How are you feeling?"

Jessica blinked up at her. "Like I've been hit by a truck."

"See this button here?" The nurse held up a small, white device attached to a tube. "It's a PCA pump that contains your pain medicine. The pump is connected through a tube to a vein in your body. You press a button when you feel pain and the pump gives you a dose of medicine set by your doctor. Don't worry about giving yourself too much because the pump will be set to prevent that. Do you understand?"

Jessica nodded, accepting the device placed in her hand. She pressed the button.

The nurse glanced behind her and then back at Jessica. "The police are here to see you. Do you feel up to talking to them? I can have them come back if you're not up for it."

"That's fine," she murmured, already feeling the effects of the pain medicine.

Owen interjected, "She just had surgery last night. Can't this wait until she's stronger?"

Jessica released her hold on that precious button and touched Owen on the hand. "It's okay. I can do this."

"Are you sure?"

"I am."

The nurse wandered over to the door and pulled it open to admit Chief of Police, Gary

Randall and Detective Vickerson from the Banbridge County Sheriff's Department.

Vickerson spoke first. "Mrs. Nobles? Are you up to answering a few questions? We'll keep it brief."

Jessica spent the next twenty minutes reliving her time with Jasper Dayton. She told the officers about Eustice and Jasper's sex trafficking business and how Terry Dayton had lost his life because of it. She also informed them of the location of Terry's grave, along with the bodies in the lake.

A brief pause ensued. Jessica met Gary Randall's gaze. "Has Melanie Dayton been told about her husband?"

Randall ran a hand down his face and then flipped his notepad closed. "That's enough for today. We'll get out of here and let you rest now."

Jessica looked from Randall to Vickerson before settling her heavy gaze on Owen. "What…is it?"

"Nothing for you to be concerned about. Get some sleep and we'll talk more when you're rested."

Jess wanted nothing more than to sleep, but something in Owen's eyes, prevented her from closing her own. "What are…you…"

Chapter Forty-Seven

Owen watched Jessica's eyes slide closed before she'd fully completed her sentence.

He released her hand and turned to follow Vickerson and the police chief from the room.

They stopped in the hall to face him.

Vickerson appeared contrite. "I'm sorry about your wife, Mr. Nobles. If it's any consolation, she's been cleared of any suspicion surrounding Sandy Weaver's death. We found the murder weapon on Jasper Dayton's person along with his fingerprints."

"I'm betting Eustice Martin's blood is on that knife as well," Chief Randall admitted.

Owen leaned a shoulder against the wall, relieved that Jess had been cleared. "What happens now?"

"Since Jasper and Eustice Martin are dead," Randall began, "there will be no need for trial. We'll get your wife's official statement once she's released, and then go from there. God only knows how many bodies we'll find at that lake."

Owen pushed away from the wall and extended his hand to Randall. "Once you have what you need from Jessica, I'll be taking her back to Chicago."

Randall accepted his outstretched palm. "I can't say that I blame you. We'll be excavating the Dayton's property and dragging the lake in search of more bodies."

"What will happen to Terry Dayton's remains?" Owen hoped the child would have a decent memorial.

"The city will be paying for his burial. I'll let you know the details of that as soon as I have them."

"I appreciate it."

Owen returned to his wife's room and pulled up a chair next to her bedside. She looked so pale and fragile lying there hooked up to all those tubes.

"I'm sorry, Jess. I'm sorry for everything."

She made a sound in the back of her throat, though her eyes remained closed.

Owen vowed in that moment to spend the rest of his life making up for his mistakes. He'd spent so many years attempting to be the strong one, when in truth, it was Jessica that held all the strength. She'd followed her heart no matter who or how many were against her...including her husband.

He reached over the railing of the bed and laid his palm over the back of her hand. "I hope you can forgive me, Jess, because if you can't, I don't know what I'll do. I promise you that I'll spend the rest of my life proving to you, how much I love you."

She didn't answer, but the fingers beneath his, lifted in the barest of caresses, telling him without words that she heard him.

* * * *

Owen remained next to Jessica at Terry Dayton's gravesite, long after the small crowd who'd attended, dispersed. He didn't speak, figuring Jessica needed the quiet to say her goodbyes.

Terry had been buried next to his mother, Melanie. Though, Owen didn't know what became of Jasper's ashes; he did know that Jasper's family had him cremated.

Steven Ruckle was laid to rest a few days after Jess had been released from the hospital. She had attended his funeral with Owen at her side.

Jessica had spent the last two weeks, healing physically, but mentally, she'd remained detached.

Not that Owen blamed her. If he'd been through what Jessica had, he would no doubt react the same if not worse.

It broke his heart to see the sadness lurking in Jessica's eyes. Even with the determination she'd exhibited, she held tight to a certain amount of insecurity.

He watched her slowly twirl the stem of a rose between her fingers before stepping forward and gingerly placing it on Terry's small coffin.

A lone tear slipped from her eye. "Fly with the angels, sweet Terry. If you happen to see my Jacob, tell him his mother loves him more than anything."

Owen's heart cracked. It took everything he had not to break down in tears next to her.

She suddenly looked up and locked gazes with him. "It's time for me to let go now."

The tears Owen tried so hard to fight, came spilling forth unbidden. He could only stare down at her, unable to find his voice.

She reached up and brushed away his tears with her thumbs. "Jacob would want us to continue — to honor him by living."

Owen finally found his voice. "Yes, he would. Forgive me, Jess. Forgive me for not being there for you when you needed me the most."

"You were always there for me, Owen. I'm the one who's been absent for the past three and a half years."

He threw his arms around her, pulling her close against his heart. "Ah, God, I love you."

She hugged him back. "I know you do, and I love you, too."

"We can go back to Chicago, Jess. I can probably get my old job back. And if not—"

"Shhhhh," she shushed him, pulling back enough to look into his eyes. "We're not going back. It's time to move forward. Our life is in Florida now. Besides, I've been researching the school system here, and I think it's time I went back to work."

Owen's breath caught. "Jess?"

She sent him a smile that reflected in her eyes. "We have plenty of time to discuss future plans. Come on, let's go home."

Epilogue

One Year Later

Jessica pushed the frilly-pink stroller down the sidewalk of Meadowbrook Circle, watching a string of kids pedal down the street on the bikes they'd obviously gotten for Christmas.

Her mind wondered back to an image she'd painted the night before of Jacob, running through a field of flowers. And on Jacob's right, ran Terry Dayton, laughter evident on his little face.

Jess inwardly smiled at the final image Terry had left her with. Jacob was at peace.

She grinned up at Owen who strolled along beside her. "Do you remember how excited Jacob was when we took the training wheels off his bike?"

Jessica could speak of their son now without shattering into a million pieces.

Though she would miss Jacob everyday for the rest of her life, she had finally learned to live again.

"I remember," Owen laughed, winking down at his wife. "He skinned his knee in the first five minutes."

A cool breeze blew through the street, lifting Jessica's hair from her neck. She inhaled the fresh air and reached for her husband's hand. "She looks a lot like Jacob, doesn't she?"

Owen peered down at his tiny daughter, sleeping in the stroller. "She really does. Only, I think she's going to have her mother's eyes."

"Hmmm, you may be right. But I hope she has yours. I love your eyes."

"I love everything about you," Owen whispered, bending down to brush his lips across hers.

Jessica straightened as they passed the Martins' house. The door opened a few inches and Gerri Martin's face could be seen in the shadows.

Jess slowed her steps and lifted her hand in a subtle wave.

The door opened a little more.

Jessica had only seen Gerri Martin once since Eustice's death. The poor abused woman had holed up in that house, lost and alone.

On the few occasions Jessica had gone over and knocked, she'd been met with silence.

Gerri awkwardly stepped out onto her porch, visibly nervous and anxious.

"Come on," Jess whispered to Owen, nodding toward the insecure neighbor.

Owen appeared uncertain. "Are you sure this is a good idea? She might blame us for what happened to her husband."

Jessica had already thought of that. "There's only one way to find out."

Turning off the sidewalk, Jessica pasted a smile on her face and pushed the pink stroller up Gerri Martin's drive.

She stopped at the steps to the porch. "Hi, Gerri. How are you doing?"

Gerri took a hesitant step forward, her gaze lowering to the stroller. "I-I'm better. I've been doing a lot of cleaning and packing up Eustice's things."

Owen cleared his throat. "We're sorry for your loss, Mrs. Martin."

"I'm not," Gerri shyly admitted, taking another step toward the stroller. "May I?"

Jessica stepped up onto the porch and eased the stroller top back. "This is our daughter."

"Oh my," Gerri breathed, her voice wobbly with unshed tears. "I never had children of my own. Though I always wanted them."

Leaning forward to get a better look, Gerri smiled, her face lighting up with unguarded joy. "She is so beautiful. What's her name?"

Jessica reached into the stroller and gently retrieved her daughter. She turned toward Gerri and laid the sleeping baby in her arms. "We named her Terri..."

~The End~

If you enjoyed The Boy in the Window, read below for a sneak peek into the pages of Enigma: What Lies Beneath – A Science Fiction/Post-Apocalyptic Thriller/Romance that will leave you reeling.

Prologue

"Abbie, wait."

Henry's voice could barely be heard over the thundering of waves crashing in the distance.

An endless stream of tears streaked down Abbie's face as great racking sobs seized her small body. Pain welled up from her chest until it became impossible to breathe. Still, she ran.

Her father's shouts faded with every step she took until they disappeared altogether.

Branches grabbed at her arms like the bony fingers of a thousand skeletons, cutting into her skin. She welcomed the sting of every scratch; anything to relieve the pain in her heart.

Her mother's cold, pale face burned behind her eyes, frozen and empty. Gone were the laugh lines, the sparkle…the life.

Abbie couldn't bear to see her mother lying in a box for hundreds of people to pass by and say words over. She might be only seven, but she was old enough to know it meant goodbye. A coffin, they'd called it. Resting place. Final.

A wail wrenched from her small chest. It ricocheted off the trees, scattering birds in different directions. She'd give anything to have wings in that moment, to fly away and never look back.

Abbie burst onto the beach without slowing. Her little legs ate up the sand as she ran straight for the water.

Memories of swimming with her mother lit through her mind in sorrowful detail. The laughter, splashing around and exploring the unknown.

A storm was coming, but she didn't care. She needed to feel her mother's presence, to beg God to give her back.

"Abbie, do you know why the ocean is salty? It's all the tears God cries when someone passes away."

"Mama, what does 'passes away' mean?"

"Well, it means when people die, they leave this earth to become angels."

"If they get to be angels, then why does God cry?"

"For the ones that are left behind who will miss them after they're gone."

Abbie sailed headlong into the waves with her sights on the second sandbar. She would swim out as far as she could to be sure her prayers were heard. If God cried enough to create an ocean, maybe He would take pity on her and give back her mother.

The weight of her skirt wrapping around her legs made it hard to move in the churning water. She used her arms to pull herself along in a rowing motion until the current became too strong, forcing her to dive under and swim. Her eyes stung from the salt, but she held them open while memories of her mother's voice whispered through her mind.

"Abbie, did you know that dolphins can communicate with humans?"

"What is commu…commu — "

"It means talk to them."

"Have you ever talked to a dolphin?

"I sure have."

"Really? What did he say?"

"He said for me to tell my daughter to stop peeing in the water where his kids play."

Her mother's tinkering laughter echoed through her heart as she fought the tide in search of the sandbar.

Abbie's arms eventually grew weary and her lungs began to burn, leaving her no choice but to kick her way up for air.

Her head broke the surface to a wall of water so high it blocked out the sun. She opened her mouth to scream a second before a powerful wave crashed down on top of her, taking her back under.

Her body spun head over heels along the Gulf floor, leaving her powerless to stop the undertow. Panic gripped her as sand scraped her face, entering her mouth and eyes. The need to breathe became too strong, and Abbie gave up the fight. *Pain. Darkness.*

* * * *

Cold. Abbie felt chilled to her bones. Her chest burned, and something was caught in her throat. A spasm gripped her and she heaved.

A voice she didn't recognize. She screamed for someone to help her, to remove the heaviness from her neck.

Something slid along her arms to her hands. Tingling warmth. Heat spread out from her palms through her stomach and legs. The shivering stopped.

"Salutem." The strange word came from a deep voice above her. Was she dead?

She slowly lifted her heavy lids and stared up into the brilliant green gaze of a teenage boy. His eyes were a color she'd never seen before, resembling a few of the marbles she'd been recently collecting.

"God?" she wheezed.

He cocked his head to the side as if he didn't understand.

She tried to lift her arm, but he held it down. His hands were covering hers, palm to palm. He tilted his head to the other side, and more tingling heat pulsed through her skin. The pain in her chest receded.

The boy peered down at her in open curiosity, similar to the way she'd seen her dog do when he spotted an insect crawling through the grass.

"Who are you?" Abbie whispered, realizing the boy had saved her life.

He glanced up at something in the distance before returning his gaze to her once again. She wondered if maybe he didn't speak English, and pulled one of her hands free of his to point at herself. "Abbie."

"Abbie," he repeated in a strange accent.

"Yes." She touched her finger to his chest. "And your name?"

Shouts could be heard over the crashing of the waves, and the boy suddenly stilled. Abbie watched in wonder as he sprang away from her and dove into the water.

She pushed up onto her elbows in time to see him swim out toward the sandbar with the speed of a dolphin before disappearing from view altogether.

"No, wait." She rose to her knees at the edge of the Gulf. Her gaze flew over every wave of the rolling water, but there was no sign of her savior. Fear gripped her, and she forced herself forward. She had to find him.

"Abbie!" her father's terrified voice shouted in the distance. "Abbie, sweetheart, don't move! Daddy's coming."

How could the boy stay under the water so long? she wondered, searching the sandbar and beyond.

Henry was suddenly there, scooping her up into his arms. "Somebody call 911!"

"Daddy, we have to help him." Abbie tried to wriggle free, but he only held on tighter.

"Help who, sweetie?"

"The boy."

Her father turned in a half circle, scanning the beach without slowing his steps. "What boy?"

"The one who pulled me out of the water."

"There's no one there, honey. And don't ever scare me like that again."

He began to run toward the dunes where a small crowd flocked in their direction with cell phones in hand.

"Is she all right?" an older woman with bright red lipstick yelled as she stumbled along the sand. But Abbie was no longer listening.

She twisted her head around, frantically searching for the boy who had magically disappeared in the great pool of God's tears.

Chapter One

Twenty-five years later

"You really should eat better, young lady. Your mother would have my ass if she were alive to see some of the dreadful things you consume."

Abbie hid a smile at her father's scolding. "I'm thirty-two years old, Henry. I doubt she would go all June Cleaver on me."

"You shouldn't call me Henry, you little brat. It makes me sound old and boring."

"If the toupee fits." They both laughed a moment before falling into a comfortable silence.

Abbie's mother had died from cancer twenty-five years earlier, and Henry had never remarried. He hid his loneliness behind a mask of indifference and immersed himself wholly in his work.

Being the lead epidemiologist for Winchester Industries had become Henry's proverbial crutch, and he spent entirely too much time alone at the lab.

Abbie worried about him constantly and planned evenings such as the one they had tonight to spend quality time together. It didn't always work. She knew he saw her mother every time he looked into his daughter's eyes. The exact replica of the only woman he'd ever loved.

The trill of a phone broke the silence and her father excused himself to take the call.

Work, no doubt, Abbie thought, taking a bite of the burger she'd just made to her liking.

He reappeared a moment later with a guilty look in his eyes. "That was the lab, honey. They need me to come back in."

"What could be so important that it can't wait until morning?"

He avoided her gaze. "I'm not sure, but I'll call you later. Don't wait up. It's going to be a late night."

Something in his voice kicked her curiosity up a notch. He never could hide things well, and the whole no eye contact? Yeah, he was definitely keeping something from her.

"I'll come with you." She pushed her plate aside and stood.

"Nonsense. Stay and eat your heart attack on a bun. You worked a twelve-hour shift at the hospital today. You don't need to be running around behind me."

Abbie had worked at Winchester Industries with her father for several years and often assisted him in the lab before she'd been unceremoniously laid off due to supposed budget cuts.

She knew the higher ups had purposefully kept things from her during her time working in the lab, but whatever Henry hid from her now had to be awfully big for him to outright lie to his only daughter.

And she had no doubt he evaded the truth by the way his left eye twitched. That little trademark had always given him away. "What are you not telling me?"

He pursed his lips. "Okay, you got me. I didn't want to have to say this, honey, but you are adopted."

A chuckle bubbled up before she could stop it. She stood on tiptoes and gave him a quick peck on the chin. "That explains a whole hell of a lot."

"You look so much like your mother, Abbigail. She had the same hazel eyes and dark hair. Her butt wasn't quite as big though."

Abbie playfully smacked him on the arm before stepping back. "I inherited the infamous booty from you, Henry."

She knew he didn't like her to call him Henry any more than she appreciated him referring to her as Abbigail. They were incorrigible teases, but it was their way.

"I really do have to run, sweetie."

"At least let me pack up your food to take with you or you won't eat."

He nodded and began gathering his work paraphernalia while she bagged up his dinner.

Abbie followed him to the car and held the door open as he deposited his things on the passenger seat.

"You are welcome to stay here tonight, Abbie. Jax would love the company."

"I probably will. If I leave, I'll feed him before I go."

He gave her a two-finger salute and slid behind the wheel.

Abbie stepped back as the door closed and the engine roared to life. He backed out of the drive without another glance in her direction.

She waited until his tail lights disappeared around the corner before going back inside to put food out for Jax.

He followed her around with a rubber ball in his mouth, bumping into her legs. The big German shepherd had been with Henry for nearly ten years and had become part of the family.

"You know what's going on, don't you, boy?"

His tail wagged in response from the attention.

"Wanna give me a clue? No? I didn't think so. You are a male after all." She snagged the ball from his jaws and tossed it across the room, grinning as he bounded after it.

After a quick shower, Abbie brushed her teeth and strolled to her old bedroom in search of something to wear. Henry kept the room exactly as Abbie had left it before she'd gone off to college, right down to the blue pom-poms hanging from the bedpost.

She dressed in a pair of jeans and a black tank top, pulled her long, dark hair back in a ponytail, and made haste cleaning up the mess from their earlier dinner.

Her gaze landed on the bag of food she'd packed him. He'd obviously forgotten it in his haste to get back to the lab.

With a sigh, she plucked up the bag, grabbed her keys and left the house.

* * * *

Abbie pulled into the parking lot of Winchester Industries and switched off the engine.

Her father's car sat in its reserved spot in front of a sign that read *H. Sutherland*. She exited the car, and glanced up at the camera situated on the corner of the building.

The evening security guard waved from his perch behind a small, less than clean window. Smudges on the glass blurred his smile, but she couldn't mistake the shiny gold tooth displayed so proudly from its position in the front of his mouth.

The door buzzed once, and a *click* told her the lock had released. She pulled it open and stepped inside.

"Hi, Willie. How are you this evening?"

Willie had been one of her favorite night watchmen. His uniform always appeared clean, neatly creased, and he smelled nice. The badge he wore shone perfectly to match the bald spot on top of his head. He had a toothy grin for everyone and a heart of gold.

"Doing good, Miss Abbie. I sure have missed your face around here. The place hasn't been the same since you were laid off."

"Thank you, Willie. I miss you too."

Willie cleared his throat. "What brings you here?"

"Henry forgot his dinner." She held up the brown paper bag for him to see.

"I hate it when that happens. My wife is always harping at me about how forgetful I'm getting. I reckon she's right. It's hard getting old. He must be working on something pretty big to bring him down here at this hour. It's almost nine o'clock."

Abbie couldn't agree more. "He's always been eager to please when it comes to

Newman. This lab has become his whole life, it seems."

Willie nodded and waved her on. "Tell him not to work too hard."

"Have a good night, Willie. Tell that beautiful wife of yours I'm ready for more of her fried chicken."

"I sure will." He beamed.

"See you, Willie." She winked at him and hurried off down the hall.

The cameras strategically placed along the corners of the ceiling caught her eye.

Abbie knew Winchester Industries pushed the limits and sometimes experimented with drugs not previously approved by the FDA. But whatever her father had rushed to the lab for had nothing to do with illegal testing. He wouldn't have been asked to come back in for that alone.

Taking the elevator up to the third floor, Abbie waited for the doors to open and stepped out into the hallway.

The door to her father's lab lay straight ahead. She trailed across the hall and turned the knob.

The predictable sounds of a lab in use met her ears as she eased the door open and entered her father's domain.

He obviously hadn't heard the door shut behind her over the consistent beeps and humming of the equipment surrounding him.

Abbie took in the room with a quick glance, noticing a big pair of feet hanging off the end of a bed her father stood next to.

Curiosity took hold as she crept farther inside. The closer she got the more confused she became. It was definitely a man lying on the bed; only, she'd never seen one that size in her lifetime.

A sheet covered his lower body from waist to ankles, leaving his upper half bare. His chest appeared devoid of hair and stood off the bed about two feet. He was massive and had to be at least six foot ten by her estimation.

Warmth enveloped Abbie as her gaze slid to the stranger's face. Beautiful would be a gross understatement.

He had a smooth, strong jaw that angled up to slightly pointed ears. *Pointed ears?*

His dark hair lay haphazardly tousled on the pillow. Full lips and a faintly crooked nose made up the rest of his face. She wondered what color his eyes were.

Without conscious thought, Abbie inched forward on shaky legs. *Why would they have him here? Is he sick?*

Her father must have sensed her approach. He stiffened a second before spinning around. "What are you doing here?"

He seemed more nervous than surprised.

"I brought your dinner. You left in such a hurry, you forgot it."

"You shouldn't be here," he snapped, reaching for the bag she held.

"What's going on, Henry?" She nodded toward the incapacitated stranger taking up far too much bed.

His face paled slightly. "You have to leave. Now."

Anxiety surged. "What is that man doing here? This isn't a hospital, so don't lie me. I knew something was going on when you got that phone call earlier. What sort of illegal activity do they have you involved in this time?"

"Honey, please. You're not supposed to be here. You need to go home. Now. I'll explain it all in the morning." He glanced toward to door several times as he spoke.

"Not until you tell me what you're involved in. You promised me you wouldn't participate in anymore illegal activities, Dad. No matter what Newman threatened you with."

Henry took a deep breath and pinned her with an impatient stare. "Fine. But then you must go. And it's not what you think. Newman didn't threaten me, but he might if he finds you here."

Abbie raised an eyebrow. "Am I not allowed up here? And Willie let me in. He doesn't know what kind of illegal dealings go on in this lab. He thinks that I was laid off due to budget cuts."

Henry averted his gaze. "You're going to be the death of me."

Chapter Two

Abbie stared at her father as he attempted to explain away the man's presence with some fabricated tale.

"This is all I know. It..." Henry took a deep breath and started again. "It washed up on the beach a few hours ago. Newman called me in to run some tests before they extradite the corpse to Area 51."

"Wait." Abbie held up a hand when he would have continued. "Newman is the CEO of Winchester Industries, not a doctor. Why would he personally call you in? And *it*?" She jerked her chin toward the bed.

Henry hesitated. "It's not human, Abbie. I don't know what it is, but I need to get these samples taken before the crew from Area 51 arrives. You have to go. No one else is to know about this."

"Not human? That's impossible." Other than the stranger's size and pointed ears, he appeared the same as any other man. "And how did he get here?"

Henry turned to a computer near the head of the bed and tapped a few keys. The screen came out of hibernation within seconds to display a chest X-ray.

"Someone ran across the thing on the beach. Apparently, it drowned somehow and floated up on shore. Local PD had the creature sent to the morgue and Newman had it delivered here. He told the police this was a Hazmat situation and needed '*him*' contained until they cleared the scene. No one questioned Newman since he owns the hospital and this lab. The cops had no idea it was an alien."

"Why would they think he's not human? Did the coroner open him up and find a little green man in residence?" She would have rolled her eyes if the situation didn't already resemble a *Twilight Zone* episode.

"Come look at this."

Abbie stood next to her father to gaze at the unbelievable evidence of a six-chambered heart. It took a moment to register the truth, but there was no mistaking it.

"How is that possible? I've never seen anything like it. Do you know what this means?" Her voice sounded strained to her own ears.

"Neither have I. And it doesn't mean anything to us. Once it leaves here, we forget it exists."

"But, Henry —"

"No." He glanced at his watch. "The crew will arrive in less than three hours to retrieve it, and then I develop amnesia. Do you understand?"

"We have a little time before they get here. Show me please? This is too amazing to be true." Several questions ran through her mind at once. She couldn't voice them all.

With a click of the mouse, another image appeared. "Do you see that?" Henry pointed to an object on the screen.

"Yes, what is it?" She leaned in to get a better look.

"The equivalent of lungs."

"But what is that?" She indicated something winged that grew from the sides of the organs.

"They're gills." His voice took on an awed tone, which she could understand. She was in the same frame of mind.

"It can't be." Yet the evidence of it mocked her from inches away.

Henry glanced up at her. "They're gills, I tell you. I saw them on the back side of his ribs.

His arms cover most of them and they wouldn't be noticeable to someone that didn't know what to look for."

"Do you realize what this implies? Gills for God's sake."

"I'm seeing similarities to humans, amphibians, reptiles, and fish here, Abbie. The heart of a fish only has two chambers, one to receive blood and the other to send it out to the rest of the body. A human heart has four."

"Notice that our blood leaves the lungs and enters the heart, while a fish's blood leaves the heart and enters the gills. And take a gander at this." Henry clicked the mouse once more.

"What in the world?" she breathed, studying the image before her.

"It's the digestive tract. I would give anything to be able to dissect it."

His excitement at the possibility of a dissection disturbed her.

Abbie glanced over at the *it* in question, and something tugged at her emotions. Some kind of beautiful creature had washed up on the beach only to be violated and sent to a place few had ever witnessed. *Area 51.*

She shuddered and turned back to the screen. "Have you ever seen anything like this before? And why six chambers instead of two or four?"

"I don't know why the six chambers. I understand that an octopus, squid, and cuttlefish have three separate hearts, so perhaps it has to do with evolution."

Pinching the bridge of his nose, he continued. "I studied tissue samples taken from an unknown subject many years ago, but I wasn't told its origin. And it had blood. This subject doesn't. Well, barely enough to fill a cup, at any rate. And there are no wounds that it could have bled out from."

"What?" Abbie was sure she hadn't heard him right.

"Come here and I'll show you." Henry took up residence on the left side of the bed as she rushed around to the right.

He lifted the creature's left arm, turning the hand so she could see both sides. "We attempted to draw blood here first. Nothing. Not a drop could be found."

Replacing the arm, he gripped the subject's chin next, tugging it to the side for her inspection. "One vein runs along here, from jaw to the bottom of the neck. Nearly dry also."

"But— "

"I'll come back to that. There's more." He dragged the sheet down to a small pink vertical scar on the creature's abdomen. "Impossible," he gasped.

"What's wrong?" Her gaze flew to her father's face." Henry had significantly paled.

"I made that incision less than an hour ago. It's partially healed. The thing is dead. I don't understand."

"Are you sure he's...gone?" Abbie couldn't bring herself to refer to him as *it*.

"No heartbeat." Henry laid two fingers on the creature's neck. "No pulse. It's dead all right."

"So how is he healing if he isn't alive?"

"I don't know. I was able to remove a small sample of something resembling blood from near the stomach cavity, but it wasn't in any of the A, B, O, or RH classes. It's an anomaly."

"Perhaps you should try giving him a universal donation to see what happens? I mean, if he's healing, he has to be alive."

"He? It's not a person, Abbie. And I'd thought of that. I was just about to try it before you popped in here and gave me indigestion. I'm running out of time. I want you gone before that crew arrives."

"Then let's hurry. I'll help."

He shot her an impatient glance. "If you're caught in here, I could lose my job."

"I won't get caught. Not if we hurry."

Henry studied her for a moment. "So, damn stubborn."

"Yet another thing I inherited from you."

"You're not too old for me to turn over my knee, young lady." He spun on his heel and left the room.

Abbie took advantage of Henry's absence to study the beautiful creature before her. His wrists and ankles were strapped down with leather cuffs attached to bands that disappeared beneath the bed.

He looked very much alive to her, with color in his cheeks and his lips slightly parted. She was certain his mouth had been closed only moments before.

Her fingers shook as she reached toward him. She gently pushed his top lip up with her thumb.

"Holy crap," she whispered, jerking her hand back as if burned. He had razor-sharp incisors where his eyeteeth should have been.

When nothing untoward happened, Abbie slowly leaned in again.

Heat instantly surrounded her upper body. She felt a soft tugging sensation that left a tingle in its wake. Her muscles relaxed without effort as something unseen moved up the sides of her face.

A deeply accented voice invaded her mind. *"Open."*

Abbie knew she should run, but the allure of the command was more powerful than her fear.

She allowed the warmth to pull her closer, never taking her gaze from his mouth, until she half lay across his massive chest with her arms on either side of his shoulders.

A gentle pressure wrapped itself around her mind, and she found herself inching toward his parted lips to hover slightly above them. His breath mingled with hers and she breathed him in. *He's breathing?*

Abbie felt as if his very spirit entered her body, traveling down her throat and circling her chest. The pressure continued to slide through her stomach and grew in strength as it reached her abdomen.

She had no desire to move even if it were possible. Her insides turned to liquid and she exhaled softly into his mouth only to draw him in again. *He's alive…*

Abbie shifted on his huge frame and stroked her fingertips down to his wrists. Though no pulse was evident, she could feel his energy, his breath teasing her lips.

On instinct, she gripped his hands and slowly turned them over until she was palm-to-palm with him. A gentle electrical current traveled up her arms, tingling, throbbing, as if it had a life of its own.

An image of herself as a child coming awake on the beach while waves washed over her legs suddenly flashed through her mind. She jerked her head back. *What the hell?*

The pulsing continued through their points of contact while Abbie held her breath, lowering her face close to his once more. Another jolt entered her palms.

"Salutem."

Where had she heard that before? She recognized it as the Latin word for greetings.

Images and voices began swirling together in a multitude of color and sound, leaving her helpless against the onslaught.

"Abbie, did you know that dolphins can communicate with humans?"

A groan slipped from her parted lips, full of pain and sorrow. *Mother.*

More current slid from his hands to hers. *"Salt from his tears." Water. Coffin. Death.*

"No," she softly moaned.

Sand. Her lungs hurt. Heat snaking through her arms and legs. "Salutem." Blessed darkness.

Abbie heard a keening sound and realized it came from her. She slowly removed her shaky hands from his and brought them to his face. "It can't be."

With unsteady fingers, she rested her thumbs on his eyelids and gently lifted. A soft gasp escaped as she stared into the emerald-green eyes of a dream she'd thought long forgotten.

Memory was swift and strong and she clung to it like a life raft on a raging sea.

She'd wondered a thousand times about the day they'd buried her mother, when the teenage boy with the strange accent and rare-colored eyes had magically appeared to save her life.

The memory had faded over the years until she'd convinced herself it'd all been the imagination of a child who'd recently suffered a trauma.

Abbie couldn't believe the boy from her dreams was actually real and strapped down before her now.

She forced herself to break the connection and stand on legs that felt too weak to hold her up. His warmth abruptly disappeared, leaving

an ache and emptiness in its place that was
staggering.

Chapter Three

Unimaginable pain. Hauke could hear his sister's scream piercing the night, ripping his heart in half. *Sunlight scorched his skin. The cool, healing power of the water.*

He could breathe once again. Voices. More pain. The distinct feel of a blade opening his skin.

His defenseless state enraged him. To be trapped inside his own mind, unable to retaliate as someone violated his body.

A female. Compassion.

Images plagued him, making little sense.

He clung to the female's voice. She touched him. He knew she attempted to soothe him, yet he couldn't read her thoughts.

"Open," he mentally implored.

Her mind became partially exposed to him as he beckoned her closer. His spirit clawed its way to the surface, craving hers. It was a hunger unlike anything he'd ever known.

Her breath entered his mouth, and he felt as if he'd died a thousand times. He saw her lovely face in its true form behind his closed lids. Soft, warm, and expressive. She cared about what happened to him.

He took in her sweet scent, amazed as his spirit encircled hers, wrapping itself around her life force in a slow, sensual slide.

The connection broke unexpectedly, and he panicked. The pain from it went beyond the physical to be felt in his soul.

Something pricked Hauke's arm, and warm, blessed liquid traveled up, straight into his heart.

It beat for the first time in hours — days… He was unsure of how long he'd been gone. If not for the membrane in the roof of his mouth producing the enzymes he needed to heal and keep his organs from shutting down, Hauke knew he would already be dead. He had no clue how long he'd been in the coma-induced sleep.

The sensation kept coming, and he realized blood somehow pumped into him. The female had to be responsible, he thought, feeling his body soak up every last drop of the coveted source.

Somewhere inside his subconscious, he knew it to be human blood now coursing through his veins. Forbidden among his kind; yet there was nothing he could do but allow it to happen.

Moisture filled his eyes in stark relief, and his protective lenses slid into place. He lifted his lids enough to see shapes moving around the room.

The female's voice sounded from somewhere near his feet, and he zeroed in on her.

She wasn't beautiful in the conventional sense, though she was still very attractive. Sensuality surrounded her. He wished she would come closer where he could see her eyes.

A beeping noise echoed around him, and someone shouted from nearby. "It's alive, Abbie! Get back."

"I'm okay, Henry. He's strapped down and not fighting."

Abbie...

Hauke's people had been familiar with the English language since the great flood over two thousand years ago. Some of the words had changed over time, but he had little trouble keeping up. Although, the couple in the room with him did have strange accents, he silently admitted.

Hauke didn't recognize the voice to his left and cut his gaze in that direction. A tall man with gray hair, wearing a white garment stared back at him with wide eyes. Hauke growled deep in his throat, registering him as a threat.

Abbie's voice broke through his defensive state. "Hello? Can you understand me?"

He brought his focus back on her, and his chest constricted with emotion. It was her. The young girl that nearly drowned in the Gulf all those moons ago.

The foreign feeling did little to slow his curiosity. He openly stared, drinking in her expressive features.

Hauke wanted to communicate with her, but the older man would hear. He sent her a thought instead. *"I comprehend."*

A small intake of air was the only sign that she might have heard him.

He tried again. *"Come."*

She slowly moved forward until she stood next to his head. The fact that she'd gone to the same side as the man wearing white wasn't lost on Hauke. *She is protecting me.* The thought warmed him.

The female had no idea how much power he possessed. The only reason he hadn't broken loose and snapped the old one's neck, stood before him now. He didn't want her to fear him.

"Abbie." He liked the sound of her name.

She appeared nervous but didn't run. There was a determined set to her jaw that he found oddly sexy.

"Move back this instant," the gray-haired one demanded from behind her. "If that thing gets loose, you could be killed. And we have no idea what type of diseases it carries."

Abbie spun around. "Just stop it, Henry. He's alive. Does he look like he's trying to break free to you? Have you no heart? We have to do something before they get here. He will die at Area 51."

"It's not our problem, Abbigail. Their crew is already on the way. There's nothing we can do."

Hauke listened to the exchange, understanding enough to know that the one Abbie referred to as Henry planned on sending him somewhere to die.

He could feel his strength returning with the help of the blood now inching through his veins. The hunger for more grew by the second and his fangs began to throb in time with his pulse.

"I'm disappointed in you, Dad."

Hauke didn't miss the catch in her voice or the parent reference. *He's her sire.* He filed that piece of information away for a later time. His first priority was to get out of there and find the group that had been with him before the explosion.

His heart ached with the knowledge that his sister might not have survived. If she'd died, he would destroy every last human involved in blowing the oil well that separated Naura from him.

"What do you expect me to do? Take it home with me and set up a college fund for it? Come on, Abbie. Be reasonable. You saw the X-rays. That thing may resemble us to a degree, but that's as far as it goes. You took a huge risk giving it blood. We have no idea what the consequences of that might be."

"Henry— "

"No," he snapped, grabbing onto her arm and tugging her away from the bed. "Now keep your distance while I check on the incubated samples. It'll be gone soon, and we have no choice but to forget we ever saw it." Henry stalked off, leaving a fuming Abbie to gape at his back.

The door suddenly opened, admitting a short, beefy man wearing dark blue clothing. Something shiny hung from his shirt. He stood there for a moment, leering at Abbie before coming fully into the room. "What are you doing here, Doctor Sutherland?"

It would appear that Abbie was a healer, Hauke noted, watching the man in blue slowly advance forward.

"My father was called in late and forgot his dinner. I just stopped by to bring it to him." She nodded toward the brown paper bag sitting next to the computer.

"Who is that behind you on the bed?"

Abbie cleared her throat. "That man is sick. I wouldn't advise you come any closer."

Hauke didn't need to open his mind to feel the nervousness in her words. They fairly dripped with it.

"Where's your father?" Donald turned toward the door Henry had disappeared through only minutes before.

"You can't go in there, Donald. He's spinning samples at the moment. You'll run the risk of contamination."

Donald nodded, peering back at her with traces of lust swimming in his eyes. "I'll be in the restroom if you need me...for anything." Donald winked at her and sauntered across the room, disappearing behind a row of bottle-filled shelves.

Hauke bit down hard enough that one of his incisors pierced his bottom lip. His stomach turned over at the man's filthy thoughts of Abbie. Hauke didn't need to touch him to read his intentions.

"Abbie." Her name came out in a whisper only to be swallowed up by the insistent noises of the room. He tried again. "Abbie."

She spun around to face him with surprise registering on her face. "You can speak."

He attempted to lift his arm, but the restraints held him back. It would be easy to break free, apprehend her, and escape. But the thought of frightening her in any way was unacceptable to him.

"*Ubi ego sum?*"

"I'm sorry. I don't understand?"

Though Latin was commonplace among his kind, Hauke spoke many languages. English had been the most difficult to learn due to the backhanded slang most humans used. The need to practice it over the years had been rare since he'd only come in contact with a small handful of them.

He cross-referenced words in his mind. "Where am I?"

"You're in a lab. Someone found you on the beach. We thought you were dead." She visibly swallowed. "Wh-what... Who are you?"

"I am Hauke. Son of Klause. What means Area 51?"

She averted her eyes. "Are you in pain?"

That would be an understatement. He ached from head to feet. Even his hair seemed to hurt. "No pain."

"You must be thirsty." She darted away before he could answer.

He would have laughed if it wouldn't hurt to do so. Any other time, he'd enjoy teasing her. Not today.

Hauke tested his bonds. *Simple.* They thought to hold him with their straps.

Abbie returned to his side, holding a clear plastic cup. He gave her a questioning look.

"It's just water."

"Something floats inside." He'd never seen its contents before.

She glanced down at the cup and her lips twitched. "That's ice. It keeps the water cold."

Her voice took on a husky tone as she leaned over him and slid her arm beneath his head. "Here, try it."

Heat and energy radiated from her in the way Hauke imagined the sun would feel on his skin in that moment.

He breathed deep, taking in her essence. Her spirit was strong and he felt his own rise to the surface, seeking a closeness with her.

A possessive growl rumbled from his chest, and she stilled.

"Do not fear me, Abbie."

"Did I hurt you?"

He only shook his head.

The sincerity in her voice made him want her more. Emotion poured from her in waves. Her concern over his pain touched him in ways he didn't understand.

She lifted his head off the pillow and brought the cup to his mouth. "Small sips."

The cool liquid touched his tongue, and he bit back a groan. Hauke drank slowly to appease her. If she had any idea he was capable of breathing underwater, she'd probably be horrified. No, he rather enjoyed her caring for him.

Her soft breast pressing against his cheek nearly drove him to insanity. He wanted to turn his face to the side and nuzzle her.

She removed the drink from his lips and eased her arm out from under his neck.

Hauke missed her touch instantly. He watched her set the cup on a side table and busy herself with the tube attached to his arm.

"Thank you, Abbie."

She blushed but didn't say anything.

"Your sire." He nodded toward the other room. "He is concerned for your safety."

"My Sire?" She gifted him with a small smile. "Where do you come from?"

He answered her with a question of his own. "What means Area 51?"

Hauke felt her emotions shift. She was like an open book with her expressive features and guileless eyes.

She hesitated. "It's a place where they... um...I have never actually been there." She appeared flustered. "Shit. You need to get out of here. "

The sound of footsteps could be heard coming from somewhere in the back. Abbie quickly put space between her and the bed. The anxiety radiating from her was suffocating.

"It's just Henry."

The whispered words did little to slow the growl rising in Hauke's throat. He didn't trust Abbie's father.

Hauke studied the older man as he progressed into the room. He was hiding something, and Hauke wondered how much of it had to do with the prize he had strapped to the bed.

"One of the samples was compromised. I'm going to need another." Henry went to a stainless steel side table and opened the drawer. He withdrew several items, laying them on top.

"What are you doing with that?" The spike in Abbie's adrenaline wasn't lost on Hauke.

"I'm going to sedate- "

"You can't do that," she interrupted.

Henry barely spared her a glance as he lifted a vial from his coat pocket and set it beside the other items on the table. "I have to sedate him to get the samples. I'm sure as hell not going near him while he's lucid."

The older man tore open something that appeared to have a miniature blade protruding from one end, and plucked up the small glass bottle in his other hand. After holding them both up to the light, he pierced the vial with the sharp point.

"I can't let you drug him, Dad. If they take him to Area 51, he'll die."

Henry raised an eyebrow. "What do you propose we do, Abbie? Let him go? We don't even know what he is or if there are others out there like him. Now, I need you to get out of here. It won't bode well for either of us if you get seen in here."

"Too late," Abbie breathed. "Donald saw me."

Henry's eyes grew round with worry before he shook his head. "It doesn't matter. Get going before he returns. I'll think of something to tell him."

Abbie crossed her arms over her chest.

Titles by Ditter Kellen

The Seeker Series

Ember - Five Book Box Set

Shon

The Rise of Vlad

Supernatural Series

Finding Carly

Bitten

Beautiful Haunting

Secret Series

Lydia's Secret

Midnight Secrets

Time Travel Series

Turn the Page

Worlds Apart-Coming Soon

Enigma Series

Enigma: What Lies Beneath

Naura

Vaulcron

Zaureth

Oz

Gryke

Braum

Rykaur

Thrasher

Zyen

Eyes Without a Face

Coming Soon as a Stand Alone

Ruby and the Beast

A Beauty and the Beast Tale

The Billionaire's Baby

A BBW Shifter Romance

Audible Titles

The Seeker Series
Ember
Shon
The Rise of Vlad

The Seeker Trilogy
Three Book Set

Enigma Series
Enigma: What Lies Beneath
Naura
Vaulcron
Zaureth
Oz
Gryke

Ruby and the Beast
A Beauty and the Beast Tale

About Ditter

Ditter Kellen has been in love with romance for over thirty years. Her eBook reader is an extension of her and holds many of her fantasies and secrets. It's filled with dragons, shifters, vampires, ghosts and many more jaw-dropping characters who keep her entertained on a daily basis.

Ditter's love of paranormal and outrageous imagination have conspired to bring her where she is today...sitting in front of her computer allowing them free rein. I hope you will enjoy reading her stories as much as she loves spinning them.

Ditter resides in Florida with her husband and many unique farm animals. She adores French fries and her phone is permanently attached to her ear. You can contact Ditter by email: author@ditterkellen.com

Follow Ditter on Social Media

Newsletter BookBub FaceBook Twitter
Website Blog Instagram

Subscribe to Ditter's Newsletter for free books, new release alerts and contest opportunities!

Sign Me Up!

46316756R10267

Made in the USA
Middletown, DE
27 May 2019